AYAAN

Pakhi

Dedicated to my Mother.

Acknowledgement

Finding Ayaan is the first and the closest story to my heart. It is a story of instinct. Believe in the abilities and let the magic find you and make you a stronger person.

There are two things a writer needs - time and the will to write.

I thank my Guruji Sri Sri for always walking beside me in each and every phase of my life.

My sweetheart, my love Atharva for feeling proud of his mumma and giving his unconditional love.

My parents for making me a stronger person and loving me unconditionally.

Amit, Gaurav, Nishit, Aakaash - thanks guys for making me believe in my abilities.

Mandira, Neha, Sushma, Tanisha, Ambreen, Durga, Sreemoyee for always standing by me.

I thank my superstar readers for purchasing a copy of this book and investing your valuable time in it. You justify my existence as a writer, and I owe my identity to you. Keep loving me as always.

Writing is a continuous learning process, and I would be even more grateful to you if you could let me know what you think of the stories.

Do send me your feedback at pakhisstories@gmail.com
Last but not the least, gratitude to my late grandparents for always being my guardian angels. I miss you Dada and Ma.

Chapter 1

❤

Abeer found Ria sitting on a large rock near the waterfall. She had her back to him. It was mid June and a hill station like Shimla was also surrounded by the warmth of the sun in the early afternoon. He left the rented four-wheeler car right in front of the parking lot and asked the driver to pick him up in 15 minutes from then. He carefully began to make his way to the waterfall area, between a fleet of school kids. As he came closer, he could see that she was fiddling with her camera.

"Ria Mehta?" Abeer's approach was so silent that at the sound of his voice, Ria went still. She slowly got up from her comfortable rock and turned. He felt an actual physical attraction when she met his eyes. Her eyes were a startling dark blue and he just couldn't take off his gaze.

Ria answered, "Yes, what can I do for you?"

Abeer replied, "My name is Abeer Singh. Your grandmother told me where to find you."

Ria inquired, "She did?"

Ria thought if granny has sent him after her, then there has to be more than the gazing of the eyes for sure. She tried studying him. He was about a foot taller than her, height 5.8 inches. He didn't seem to be from the mountains as he was wearing an expensive suit and shoes which normally no one wears on the mountains. He was surely from a big city. She spoke, "Granny must have liked your voice."

Abeer questioned, "Who? What?"

Ria clarified, "I mean… granny never told me about you. She wouldn't send a stranger after me unless….. Well Mr.

Singh, did granny invite you to my house? Ok, so here I am, tell me, what do you want from me?"

Abeer answered, "Ms. Mehta, I am here to consult a psychi…."

Ria interrupted, "I don't believe it. You have come to take my help? You believe in all this? A man like you shouldn't be here running after a psychic. A man like you who doesn't believe in them."

Abeer said coldly, "A man like me doesn't come all the way to your small town without a reason madam." He was inclined to her gaze. He knew she was searching for something… some clue that would give his motives away. He now understood how these intuitions work. They depend more on observations than on any real mystical powers.

He said, "I have heard you have succeeded in finding some missing people."

Ria was now irritated. She knew Abeer really wanted her guidance but he was self guarded and would not tell her the full truth. She walked off the rock and said, "I don't know why exactly you are here and you are not even telling me." While walking off, she stumbled and Abeer caught her from falling off. Sparks triggered widely beneath her fingers and she stopped and looked at him scared. Abeer knew she wouldn't accept any dishonesty from him. He very well had cultivated these manners and immediately apologized to her. He just couldn't afford to let her distance from this assignment. He had to get his nephew back. He told her that his sister Aarti had heard about her and hence he came to meet her. He also mentioned about his nephew Ayaan who has been missing for a week now and all the search investigations have failed him miserably.

She shut her eyelids and was prepared for the flood of emotions that filled her while taking the child's name in her mind.

She tried hard but there was nothing that could be useful. The emotions rolled over her and she knew she won't get any information unless she gets hold of Ayaan's belongings to regain her focus. She opened her eyes and saw Abeer standing in front of her. She felt uneasy. He was dangerous – her instinct told her. There was something more to him that gave her electric reactions. She wasn't behaving normal in front of him. Suddenly, she started walking away.

Abeer called out, "Hey, wait a minute. Where are you going?"

Ria replied, "I am going home. You meet me there."

Abeer suggested, "I have my car. Come along, I'll give you a lift."

Ria held her long white dress with one hand and her camera with the other and started running down in between the lanes and small houses. Expressionless, Abeer ran to his car and told the driver to follow the lady. He knew Ria was frightened by his actions and he promised himself to be more careful with her. He felt she was a fake but if she could be of any help in the search for Ayaan, he won't mess with her again.

Ria reached her house and barged in. She called out, "Granny, it's me." Granny replied, "I know dear – who else would bang the door while entering the house." Ria checked the cookies that her granny had just removed from the oven and popped one in her mouth.

Ria said, "Abeer Singh found me."

Granny said, "As soon as I heard him, I knew it's him. He needs your help Ria. He is totally helpless and I know you'll surely unwind the truth for him." Ria never questioned her granny's visions. She trusted her completely. This was one of the reasons she felt more comfortable with her grandmother than anyone else. Ria wrapped her arms around herself as she felt a shivering sensation. The memory was still fresh in her mind.

Ria said, "He says he does. There's something about him. He is not telling me everything. All I understood was that he didn't want to come here. But there is something more than that."

Granny asked, "What more Ria?"

Ria replied, "He made me uneasy and then he touched me."

Granny inquired, "Ohh.. did you see anything?"

Ria clarified, "No, not the way you think. It was different than usual. Everything jumbled inside me. It was like touching a bare wire and getting a shock."

Ria heard the sound of a car in her driveway and opened the door to her house, knowing well it would be Abeer.

Abeer asked, "Hope your grandmother won't mind me coming in."

Ria (smiling to herself) replied, "Oh.. she would love to have a look at your chin and hear your voice." Abeer asked in surprise, "My chin?"

Ria, amused with herself, said, "Actually granny can say about a person's character just by his chin and his voice. You'll soon know."

Granny said, "Please get him in Ria and make him sit. I'll take a few minutes to wash the mess in the kitchen."

Abeer was escorted by Ria in the living room where he made himself comfortable on a cane sofa. He noticed there were beautiful pictures clicked by Ria framed on the walls. He thought to himself, 'What a waste of talent! A small town girl can never think big.' He made himself comfortable and waited.

Granny questioned, "Yes Mr. Abeer Singh… what brings you here from your busy life?"

Abeer answered, "My nephew has been missing. My sister has heard of Ria and asked me to come and see if she could help." Granny nodded. Age had surely dimmed her eyes but it was difficult to guess her age. She was super active and the glow showed on her face. She asked him, "And what do you do?"

Abeer replied, "I run a security firm Ma'am.I and my partner Saket started it around 8 years back."

Granny asked, "Security… hmm. And why didn't your sister come to meet Ria?"

Abeer answered, "Aarti, my sister had taken Ayaan to the park in his stroller. Suddenly she was pricked by someone from behind and since then she has been in the hospital due to overdose of the drug that was injected. She told me about Ria in the hospital and so I came. I have told you everything. Now will you help me?"

Granny looked at Ria and told her to decide. Ria nodded to Abeer and said, "I need some belongings of Ayaan to hold."

Abeer asked, "But for what?"

Ria answered, "This is how I work. I need to hold one of his belongings, something that was too dear to him and he kept with him most of the time. Then I may sense something about him or get a clue that will help you find him."

Abeer said, "But I am not carrying anything of him. I had no clue that you'll need one. And by the time I travel back and fro, Ayaan might go too far from us. I am even scared to think about this." Suddenly an idea struck him and he said, "Well, why don't you come along with me to Ayaan's house and pick all that you require. You may also meet Aarti for further details. She'll be glad to see you in action."

Ria was speechless as she didn't know what was coming up. Her granny was too reluctant to send her though she really wanted the little boy to be back home. But no way she would send Ria to the victim's house. This can be dangerous. She left this on

Ria to decide what she wanted to do and waited. She went dumbstruck. She just looked at Abeer and then at her granny and then again at Abeer.

Abeer said to Ria, "Do you really think after all that we are going through, I'll mislead you? My sister is in the hospital and my nephew is missing. I am not here to play a game. I request you to come along so that things can become faster. This will help all of us to finish the task. Please try to understand what we are going through."

Ria stared at him. There was something about him that disturbed her. But this time she knew he was being honest to her. If she refuses to go with him to Ayaan's house, she will never be able to forgive herself. Granny took her hand in hers and at once the strength flowed to Ria and calmed her.

Granny assured, "Ria, my child. Don't worry. Just do what your heart says. You will always do the right thing and everything will be fine."

Ria turned towards Abeer and said, "Alright, I'll come with you."

Abeer was really happy to hear this and at once he called his Manager and made the arrangements to travel from Shimla to Mumbai. Hearing the name of the city, Ria got scared. How will she stay in such a big busy city and that also with this arrogant man who didn't even trust her!

Ria rushed into her bedroom followed by her grandmother.

Granny suggested to Ria, "Get your clothes out and fill the box up. Abeer doesn't seem to be a man with patience."

Ria was in no mood to disobey her grandmother. She asked her granny, "What do you think granny? What is he?"

Granny replied, "His chin is strong and this shows he is a man of his words. If he wants something, no matter what, he finds a way to get it. But you'll be safe with him. He is a man of dignity."

Ria said, "But he thinks I am a fake granny."

Granny pointed out, "Whether Abeer agrees or not, he needs you. It's a fact. He needs you more than he knows."

Ria was full of thoughts of Abeer. She asked her inner-self, 'What else can I help him with other than helping him in the search of his nephew?' But there was no answer to it. She gave up and walked out of her room with her travel box.

Granny whispered to Ria, "Trust me child. This man needs you in many more ways than just the search. But, be careful."

Ria smiled at her granny and assured her of her safety. Granny felt sad as her child, full of talent and energy, was too innocent for the real world. Granny looked at Abeer and she knew though he seems to be a stubborn and a hard man, he is not evil and will take good care of Ria.

She told him, "Mr. Singh, do take good care of my child." Abeer felt strange but nodded in assurance.

Ria hugged her granny and bid her goodbye, promising to call her as soon as she reached Ayaan's house. Suddenly, granny with a stern voice, warned Abeer, "Abeer Singh, if you hurt my child, you are answerable to me. Be careful."

Abeer, without answering, sat in the car along with Ria and the 'Dangerous Journey' began.

Chapter 2

Ria sat quietly for a while in the car. Then she switched on the music and shut her eyes. This irritated Abeer and he switched off the music. She met his gaze and then turned away thinking that it's going to be a never ending journey for her. She asked him if they could stop somewhere for a bite as she had missed her lunch and was hungry. But Abeer didn't care to stop and they reached the airport. He told Ria to hurry up else they'll miss the flight. How Ria wished this to happen but then it won't be fair on the little boy who had been taken away from his mother. She sat next to him in the plane and fastened her seat belt. Though they were traveling in the business class and had enough space, she still clinched in her seat. Her fingers trembled. Abeer noticed her weird behaviour.

Abeer said to Ria "Ria, once the flight takes off, you can eat as much as you like. The attendant will soon be here with the menu card and you can choose what you wish to eat."

Ria replied, "No thanks, I am not hungry."

The flight took off and to Abeer's surprise Ria started trembling. Her face went pale. The plane was now in the mid-air. As soon as the seat belt sign was removed, she went to the rest-room and locked herself there. She washed her face and took long deep breaths to overcome her fears. She didn't want Abeer to sense her weakness. The flight was about to land and she came out to take her seat. The landing was swifter than the take off but it didn't help Ria much.

She was still white and pale.

Abeer inquired, "By any chance, are you afraid to fly?"

Ria answered, "Afraid? Of course not." But Abeer could sense her fears.

They reached the luggage belt and Ria felt uneasy, seeing a huge crowd near the belt. She told Abeer that she would wait in the corner for him as she doesn't want to be touched by anyone. Abeer nodded. He got both his and Ria's luggage and went to the place where she was standing. Seeing her pale face, he knew she would faint anytime and so he didn't let her carry her luggage out of the airport. They sat in the car and drove off.

****

The drive to Ayaan's house was like an energy pill to her. She rolled the window down and let the breeze hit her face. Abeer checked her out from the corners of his eyes. She looked so beautiful and innocent with her eyes shut. Her long black hair hitting her lips, made him skip a heart-beat. He so badly wanted to brush them away.

He changed his gaze to the other side as he didn't want to mess with her. He just wanted to reach home and finish making her meet Aarti, who had been discharged a few hours back from the hospital and was now resting at home. Once all this was done, he would send her back the very next day to the mountains from where he had found her.

Ria opened her eyes as she felt the car slowing down. Abeer stopped the car near a huge white gate. He came out of it and pressed a few numbers on a bar and then repeated the same. The door flung open. He got back to the car and drove inside.

Ria was shocked to see a huge driveway followed by a beautiful garden that led to the most beautiful house she had ever seen.

Abeer stopped the car and gestured to Ria to come out. But she sat still. There were guards who at once opened the car and took out the luggage.

Ria asked, "You sure you live here?"

Abeer replied, "This is where Aarti and Ayaan live."

Ria suddenly looked worried. She asked Abeer whether it would be okay if she told the truth to Aarti. Confused, Abeer wanted to know what was the truth she was talking about.

Ria said, "Many times, people don't want to listen to the harsh truth. It can be anything. Ayaan may be alive and he may be....."

Abeer said, "Noooo waysss. You will not say anything like this ever to Aarti."

Ria told him, "I don't lie to my clients."

Abeer told Ria, "You will get out of this car and come inside the house, only if you promise me that you won't say anything like this to her."

Ria nodded and said, "You can be the one to decide how to tell her." Abeer was shocked. He just stared at her. They went inside the house.

Saket and his wife Sheela welcomed them. They had been looking after Aarti as Abeer had gone to look for Ria. Saket informed them that Aarti is still sleeping and they shouldn't wake her as she has gone too weak and needs rest.

Sheela said, "It seemed a long journey for both of you. I'll get you both something to eat first and then you can both rest for a while."

Abeer said coldly, "Not needed. Ria is not hungry. She just wants to finish her assignment and leave. Uh.. Saket, did you get what's required by her?"

Saket carrying a teddy bear, "Yes, here it is."

He gave it to Ria and told her that this teddy was Ayaan's best toy ever. Ria took the teddy and shut her eyes. She was well aware of the emotions she was about to go through. She felt the soft fur of the teddy and tried hard to see something. There were emotions, but only of the present. She held the teddy tightly, trying hard to see the visuals, but nothing came up. She frowned unconsciously and opened her eyes.

Ria said, "I am sorry but I couldn't see anything. Can I have some clothing of Ayaan, it might help me. I want to try again."

Abeer said, "I guess your powers left you Miss… You need a new spell to work on now."

Ria spoke, "If I had one, I would surely change you into a human being."

"What's happening?" came a voice. Everyone turned around and saw Aarti standing. She came upto Ria and gave her a warm hug.

Aarti said, "Thank You so much Ria for coming here. One of my aunts told me about you. You had helped her neighbour locating her lost husband in the Gujarat flood a year back. I am sure you'll be able to locate my Ayaan too.

But why are you holding that teddy? Is it yours?"
Speechless, Ria understood the game plan of Abeer and stared at him.

Ria said to Aarti, "Aarti, can I please have something of Ayaan which is too dear to him. I'll be able to sense him and this will help me in his search."

At once Aarti asked Abeer to get Ayaan's favorite toy and hand it over to Ria. This toy had been too dear to Ayaan and was gifted by Abeer when he first took his nephew in his arms. From that time, Ayaan slept everynight holding the toy in his hand.

Ria took the toy from Abeer and shut her eyes once again. Images at once started flooding her mind. It was like a movie going on in her mind. 'She could see a toddler… he was sitting on a huge bed and was getting fascinated by a blue light… he was smiling at the light and wanted to hold it… whenever the kid tried to hold the light, a huge hand would grasp him and push him back to the middle of the bed…'

Ria felt the familiar pain in her temples, her neck was hurting and her back started paining but she still tried concentrating on her visions. 'The room filled with the cries of the little boy. He was lonely. Ria trembled, feeling the fear of the child. Her head started spinning and the visions started getting blur.' She felt too heavy and it was difficult for her to open her eyes. A small glimpse of light made her temples heavy with pain. It felt as if someone had been hammering and the pain turned into a devil.

Aarti asked, "Did you see something? Did you see him?"

Ria replied, "I saw a small boy with dark hair and his uncle's chin…."

Aarti said excitedly, "Ayaan…Ayaan….She 'll find him. I know she will."

Abeer said, "Aarti, please rest. Don't take so much stress."

Aarti spoke, "Abeer, Ayaan will be found. She knows where he is….."

Abeer held her, as she passed out. He carried her to her room, made her have some water and the nurse injected her to get her some relief. Abeer, who had been blaming himself for not taking good care of his sister and nephew, went out of Aarti's room to face Ria.

Ria, on the other hand, could not bear the pain in her temples. Her mouth went dry and eyes started getting moistened. She opened her handbag with shaking fingers, took out a small box that held a few relief tablets. She took out 2 tablets and swallowed them dry as fast as she could. The box in her hand fell on the floor and she too fell down with a thud.

Sheela ran towards her to help but by the time she reached, Ria had fainted. Sheela called Saket and with great difficulty, they picked Ria and made her lie on the nearest sofa. Nearly after four to five hours of deep rest, Ria opened her eyes. She saw Abeer standing right in front of her. Slowly she got up and sat, still feeling heavy at her temples.

Abeer came and sat beside her. He made sure there was enough space between the two as he didn't want any further issues with her. He spoke, "My sister believes you. She doesn't know you are giving her a fake lead."

Sheela said, "Abeer please let her complete what she wanted to tell us before Aarti collapsed. We need to know all that she visualized."

Sheela looked at Ria with hope and gestured to her to continue.

Ria said, "Ayaan is at a motel. There are 2 people with him. There is one lady for sure. But the other person – I really don't know. All I could see was his hand when he pulled Ayaan on the bed. The kid is very scared and lonely. He is just crying and……"

Abeer said, "What proof do we have that this lady is telling the truth? There is nothing rational in what she just said. Ayaan is in a motel…. Which motel… how will we find out which place is he exactly in? Nothing makes sense. She just faked about the chin and you all believe her now."

Ria said, "I am not faking Mr. Abeer. I know where he is. I know which motel he is in. I could see a picture framed near the bed. It had a picture of a motel with the name printed 'The Lion's Den'. He is there."

Saket looked at Abeer and then at Ria. He wanted to help but with just the name of the motel, how will they ever find out the location. He gestured to Abeer to start the action. But Abeer just stared at Ria.

Abeer warned Ria, "Look, you lady. Don't you mess with me. If this is fake, you'll feel sorry for yourself."

Sheela told Abeer, "Stop scaring her and find out the truth, Abeer."

Abeer gave Ria a dirty look and followed Saket out of the house.

Sheela noticed that Ria was about to pass out again. She told her to rest there until she gets her something to eat. She then went to the kitchen to order the staff.

Ria felt very weak and her temples still gave her a bad headache. She thought about Abeer. 'Abeer was hard but where his sister was concerned, he was totally a different man. He had no mask on him. But why did he carry this mask? What made him so hard and arrogant?'

Abeer and Saket sipped their coffee. It was 1 am and they were still waiting for the call. Abeer had told the cops to check the motels. But he didn't trust them so he had sent his security team for the search too. If Ria's visions really existed, today Ayaan would come back. He first needed to know if the motel actually even existed.

The phone rang. It was the head security agent to whom Abeer had assigned the search. He told Abeer that the motel did exist. The location was Singapore. Abeer hung up the phone and stared at it for sometime. He told Saket all that the agent told him.

Saket said, "Singapore! That's where Aarti's husband stays. That's where after so many years you found her. Abeer, if this is the truth, then brother we are in a big mess."

Abeer didn't know what to say. He sat on the sofa and looked up at the ceiling. He remembered everything...

'Aarti and his parents were always fighting. They were never happy together and one day his mother committed suicide, leaving her two children on themselves. She knew their father would be of no help to them but she just couldn't carry anymore and went into a deep sleep after taking a few pills. Their father, after a few years, met with a road accident. He took his last breath on the roads of Mumbai. Since then Abeer has looked after his sister. He made a great living for both of them. He inherited a huge property from his grandfather who also gave him money to stand on his feet. Aarti met Saurav at a friend's place and since then they had been together. Abeer was quite against Saurav as he knew his affection towards Aarti was only for her money. And one day, Aarti left the house. She took all the jewels and cash with her. Abeer's search for his sister had failed drastically but he never gave up. After 4 years, he found out where Aarti lived with Saurav, who was now her husband.

Aarti had loved Saurav with all her heart. But her husband's abusive behaviour always let her down. He used to beat her. He bullied her. He controlled her. And one fine day, she called Abeer and told him she wanted to get away from Saurav. At once, Abeer helped her escape the country, away from her past, away from Saurav. Aarti was carrying her child. It was her child and she wanted to save the life inside her. Abeer had her hidden for months until Ayaan was born. Ayaan's birth gave her a new life, a new hope and she forgot all the horrible days that ever existed in her life.'

Abeer thought, 'Why was he back? Did he want revenge? Was he after their money? If he wanted the money, then by now they would have received a ransom call. But then does he want Aarti back?' His mind wasn't working. Aarti and Saurav were still man and wife. They had not got divorced yet. But Abeer would never let Aarti go back to that heartless man ever again.

****

Abeer and Saket still didn't find a way to correct themselves as to if and why Saurav has taken Ayaan away. Saurav didn't even know about Aarti's pregnancy when she escaped his prison. If Saurav did trace her, he would have surely bargained with Abeer.

Abeer kept marching to and fro in the drawing room. He called his security agent and asked him to alert the Singapore police on the same. He wanted a search at the motel and would do all the needful that was required by the authorities.

Saket, still sipping his black coffee, said, "If Ria's prediction is correct then I tell you Abeer, she can be of great help to us."

Abeer said, "Are you out of your mind? She is nothing but a bluff. She must have read about the motel somewhere and gave us the name. I must tell you, she is a smart physic and nothing more than that. Soon a phone call will clear all our doubts and I'll throw her back to the mountains where she belongs. I'll prove it to you Saket.. soon.. really soon."

Saket asked, "And what after that?"

Abeer replied, "Well, then we'll still have to look for the kidnapper."

Aarti was able to sleep that night due to the relief injection that was given to her. Ria too was sleeping soundly. Abeer checked on her and saw her curled up in a blanket provided by the staff. She looked like a princess with dark eyelashes and long black hair, a few strands of which were coloured golden. Girls really wear such stuff to draw attention and a pretty looking girl does get the gaze. Not that he was against all this, he did have a great social life and have had lots of women drooling over him. Some wanted to sleep with him for money and some wanted the ever lasting relationship with him. And he, being Abeer, had nothing to give them. If he had met Ria some other time, he would have surely given her a chance. But then on a second thought, she was unlike him. He liked sophisticated and emotionally controlled women and Ria was far away from his likes. She was a woman who could never have control on her emotions and her face was easily read by others. She was full of temper and it was easy for anyone to alarm her. Looking at her one more time, Abeer sat at the nearby chair and waited for her to open her eyes.

Ria, woke up. After the usual stretches, she slowly sat up and her eyes widened seeing Abeer right in front of her, sitting on a chair.

Abeer spoke, "I think you had a good sleep."

Ria gauged at Abeer.

He looked polished. He was wearing a casual set of clothes unlike yesterday. He appeared to have taken a shower and was all set for the day.

Ria asked, "Did you find out about the motel?"

Abeer got up from his seat and sat next to Ria. He looked at her hair. He bent and lifted a strand of her hair where it was settled and rubbed it between his thumb and index finger. She went breathless. Slowly he curled the strands. She kept gazing at him and felt little shivers in her belly. Suddenly he looked at her and looked deep in her eyes. For the first time, he had no mask with her. Her gaze went to his mouth. His well shaped lips went all dry. And her lips went too close to his. The phone rang and the spell vanished. Ria turned her gaze and Abeer went still.

Saket came in and informed Abeer that the police had called. Abeer detangled his finger from her soft silky hair and stood up. He left the room with Saket.

Ria started breathing. Abeer's presence always made her jump and today it seemed as if there was some magnetic power that got them together. He had been too smooth with her and for once he behaved as a human. She felt relieved that he was no longer beside her. She noted her suitcase and got out the necessities. She was all set to start the search again after a nice soothing shower.

After her shower, Ria dressed up in loose cotton pants and a top. She checked herself in the mirror and wore some light makeup. Then she highlighted her lips with her favorite red lipstick and smiled at her reflection. After making a high pony out of her silky long hair, she went to the kitchen to bury herself with some breakfast. Aarti, Abeer, Saket and Sheela were already sipping their coffee when Ria entered the kitchen.

Abeer informed his sister Aarti, "The police have checked the motel. They didn't find anything fishy there. They have also questioned the motel staff but there is nothing that can be helpful to us. They didn't find Ayaan there."

Aarti still had hopes. She told Abeer to visit the motel and check. She couldn't trust the police. She wanted Abeer to check with Ria. She wanted Ria to accompany Abeer.

Ria went still. Her heart sank as she thought about the morning incident with Abeer.

But she had no choice and agreed to travel again with him…to the motel… in Singapore.

Chapter 3

Ria clenched the arm rest. She hated the fact that in two days, she was flying for the second time. She breathed deeply but could not help herself in waiving off her fears. She gave a glance to the man sitting beside her. How she hated him, though she had known from the beginning, he was a threat to her. But she had never thought in the physical sense. She wanted to know the reason behind the morning session that they had. But to get her facts right, she'll have to touch him and ponder on her unconscious abilities. She had spent too many years trying to shield herself from human contacts. The thought of even touching Abeer made her shiver and her body go weak. Even the most casual touches would get her emotional floods and she was still not ready for it. The few touches that she could not avoid of Abeer's, had evoked powerful currents in her. And there was no way she would invite them again. She had no reason to do so. The only thing she was sure about him was, he still believed she was a fake.

Abeer glanced at Ria sitting by his side. She had not spoken a word since they left home, not on the way to the airport and not once they boarded the flight. He knew she was not accustomed to this. By now he understood her well. He noticed her pale face. Their eyes met and he gave her a concerned smile. She turned the other way. She didn't want to be trapped again.

Abeer said, "You don't look fine to me. It seems you'll pass out any second."

Ria said, "Thanks for your concern. This is how you please a woman right? I saw your abilities sometime back at Aarti's house."

Abeer said, "So you know a lot about me? I am sure your physic powers must have told you all this. So what more do you know about me? And how does it concern you how I am?"

Ria just stared at him and spoke, "I care a damn about you Abeer. All that matters to me is that I am helping you find your nephew. You don't even trust me and I am here with you travelling to a different country."

Abeer said, "Yes of course. I do believe in your abilities to fake the people in telling their future just to make a living out of it."

Ria, trying hard to match him with her words, said, "Oh really…!!! That's why you came looking for me… You wanted my help and that's why I am here, sitting beside you in this goddamn flier and being treated like a fraud."

Abeer got annoyed and cautioned her, "Be careful with your words lady. I am warning you."

The attendant came and gave them food packages.

Abeer asked, "Anything else you want to tell me or can I have my food peacefully?"

Ria answered, "Yes, I have more to tell you. Now you need to be careful with me as I don't like to play games unlike you."

Abeer said, "And you need to know that any game I play, I only play to win."

Suddenly there was an unspoken silence between them.

After a while, Abeer looked at her. He saw her sitting still, with her eyes looking straight. She was all pale and was trying hard to breathe. At once he put his one hand on the back of her head and the other on her shoulder and shook her. He called the attendant asking him to help her with the oxygen mask. And then he saw her taking long deep breaths under the mask as she regained herself. She took off the mask and stared at him. Her eyes went heavy as she shut them. The colourful sparks were back and she could see him. Yes, it was him in his early teens.

'He was yelling, crying and there was no one to hug him. He looked around for help but all he could see were the walls in the house. There was no one. He held his baby sister in his arms and with shivering fingers touched a lady on the bed. The lady was in deep rest. He pleaded with the lady to wake up but she didn't move. He called out to her but she slept peacefully. He had lost her…yes she was his mother. He wiped his tears off and walked out of the room with his sister.'

Yet again her temples started hurting and she felt weak. Her eyes flung open and she clenched into her seat. Their eyes met. He slowly moved his hand from her shoulder and touched her cheek.

His thumb was now soothing her soft lips.

All she could voice out was, "Don't touch me Abeer."

****

Abeer and Ria reached Singapore airport and walked past the airport entrance to the car Abeer had rented. He kept the luggage inside. He then took out a map and asked Ria to guide him while he drove. Ria took the map and gestured to Abeer, the way to the motel.

Ria asked, "So what's the plan?"

Abeer replied, "I have asked Singapore police for help. They have agreed to it and have assigned a cop to me. He shall be reaching the motel itself and hopefully must have completed his search by now. If Ayaan is there, we'll get to know soon."

Ria wanted to ask more questions to him, but she was scared to put him back in the pool of sorrows that reflected in her visions when he had lost his mother. She preferred keeping quiet for now. Abeer's mind kept telling him he was being fooled. The woman beside him is a bluff and he is just wasting his time out here. But his heart wanted to believe what she revealed. He wanted Ayaan to be there, at the motel. How he wishes he finds the little boy and takes him back to his sister.

The drive took more than two hours and none of them said a word to the other during the journey. They reached the motel 'The Lion's Den' and Abeer at once went inside. Ria followed him. Abeer and the cop who was waiting for him, were in a deep conversation. She went to the reception counter and asked the lady, "How many rooms are vacant?"

Lady at the counter, "We just have 2 empty rooms. One is cleaned and ready to be occupied. The other room shall soon be done." Ria gave her a warm smile and left the counter. Without wasting a second, she went to check the empty rooms. She spotted a cleaner who was about to enter a room and followed him. It was an empty room and as soon as she stepped in, she was surrounded by a funny feeling. The cries of the child echoed. She shut her eyes yet again. She could clearly see Ayaan crying, he wanted to be in the arms of his mother.

"What are you doing here Ria?" She opened her eyes and saw Abeer.

Ria said, "Ayaan was here. I can feel his presence."

Abeer said, "Ria, give it up. There's no point. You are only making things worse for us."

Ria said, "My senses, my abilities cannot fail me. I know he was here. You have to believe me… AYAAN WAS HERE." Sudden shivers made her weak and she barged out of the room leaving all the thoughts behind.

Abeer was dumbstruck. He knew it's not possible. The motel staff and the police had all searched and came to the conclusion, there was no child in the motel. But to satisfy himself, he searched the room thoroughly. He opened the drawers and the cupboard. There was nothing.

He said loudly, "So now it is time for her to be packed and parcelled." He was just leaving the room when his eyes fell on a dustbin and he saw……

He ran out of the room, out of the hotel in search of Ria. 'How did she do it… how…', was all his mind repeated.

After roaming down a few lanes, he spotted her in a pizza hub. The table had 2 huge pizzas, some fries, a coke and a chocolate pastry, all for Ria to pamper her hunger. Abeer came and shared her table. He saw her opening her bag and taking two painkillers.

After a minute he said, "So you ordered for me too. Hmm.. you knew I'll hunt you down."

Ria said, "I am eating so keep your hands away."

Abeer said, "Alright. I am sorry for being rude in the room but how did you know?"

He told her he saw a milk bottle in the dustbin. But there are kids who use them even at a bigger age. So there was no proof of it being Ayaan's. Ria kept stuffing herself, expressionless. She wanted her filling as it would strengthen her.

Once done, she looked at him straight into his eyes and spoke, "If you want, you may leave the country. I am staying back as I need to find him."

Abeer questioned, "Are you insane? There's nothing left now. I just want you to pack off to your mountains."

Ria asked, "Why are you so stubborn? Why don't you accept it? Mr. Abeer Singh…we both know that I am the only source through which you can get your nephew back."

Abeer replied, "If you think, the little scene in the motel room proved something, you are wrong lady."

Ria said, "Fly off. I'll stay back."

Abeer spoke with great anger, "You lost. So now what the hell do you want from me? Ah ha! I get it now. I'll pay you double your fees. Just leave."

Ria said sternly, "You frustrated man! Keep the money to yourself. I don't need anything from you. I'll continue the hunt as I promised your sister to get her boy back to her. I am sick and tired of you, of your presence, of your rudeness. I don't need to leave, it's YOU who needs to get lost."

Ria got up from her seat, thanked the café owner and left for the motel. Abeer sat still. He didn't know what to do with Ria. He tightened his fist with anger. Seeing this, the café owner got him a glass of chilled water to ease him. Abeer saw him staring at him. He raised his brows to him.

The café owner said, "It's not always that I see dark hair, brown eyed men here. But surprisingly, I have noticed two such people with the same coloured hair and eyes in the past three days. In fact, your chin too matches his."

Abeer's mouth went dry. The café owner continued, "But there's a hell lot of difference between the two of you. You have been yelling at your girl and the little boy has been crying, even though his mother cuddled him."

Abeer stood up speechless. He turned to leave and saw Ria standing at the counter and paying her bills. She came back to the café as she had forgotten to pay for her meal in a hurry and overheard the conversation. But she didn't utter a word. Without a word, they both checked into a hotel nearby and went to their respective rooms. But Ria, without letting Abeer know, went back to the motel and bribed the motel worker. The worker told her she had heard the cries of a child from the room and had reported the same at the reception. But they didn't take any action and told her to keep away from the room. The darkness grew deep and she went back to her room, to the hotel.
****

Abeer shut his eyes in pain. He thought about Ayaan and Aarti. He blamed himself for the loss of Ayaan in Aarti's life. He could not give security to his nephew exactly the way he couldn't to his mother. He had failed miserably as a son, as a brother and now as an uncle. He rubbed his hands on his face with frustration and anger. He had to get rid of Ria. She had been giving false hopes to Aarti and he just couldn't stand it. He called up Saket and told him to tighten the security at his place as Saurav might be involved in the kidnapping and if this is true then surely he'll be dangerous to Aarti.

Abeer had to confront Ria. He left his room and headed for the room adjacent to his. He saw the room was not shut properly and entered it. He stalked to her bedside. She was sleeping peacefully. Her black long hair shone in the darkness of the night. He could see her profile under the blankets. He had always found her appealing and did have an urge to touch her, to feel her, to make her moan.

Abeer called out, "Lady, wake up." She kept sleeping.

Abeer pulled her blankets off her and said again, "Ria get up."

Ria shifted in the cold bed. Abeer felt heat waves in his stomach. He saw her changing position in the sleeveless satin strappy nightwear which went above her knees as she shifted. He sat next to her, on the bed. His fingers touched the fair flesh above her breast. She started getting strings of colours in her sleep and woke up screaming, "It wasn't your fault. You were just a kid. How could you have known about your mother's distress? No. Don't blame yourself. You are at no fault…."

Abeer moved his hand from her and stood up, shocked. Their eyes met. He passed the blanket to her and gestured to her to cover herself.

Abeer asked, "Who are you? How do you know? Why are you in my life?"

Ria looked down. She was in her own world. She had never been touched by a man. Gaining all the strength, she said, "It's still dark outside. Why are you here? What do you want? Abeer? Tell me… please. Tell me everything…."

Abeer took a deep breath and told her all about Aarti and Saurav. Though he didn't trust her, but today he wanted to talk to her, he wanted her to know his deep dark secrets.

He told her Saurav might have plotted the kidnapping though he has no clue of Ayaan's existence. He also told her that Saurav was a musician and played drums and that he lived here, in Singapore and worked as a coach in Day Dreamer's Academy. Abeer's eyes fell on her as she got the blanket closer to her cold body. He apologised to her, "Sorry for waking you up at this odd hour," and left the room.

It just took Ria a few seconds to make her way to her dreams while Abeer lay awake on his bed for hours till his tired eyes gave him some rest.

Chapter 4

Ria started filling the form and wrote the preferred instrument she wanted to learn. After putting all the information, she handed the form with a photograph of hers to the academy counselor. The counselor was surprised to find that Ria was keen to learn drums. She shrugged and told her to wait for the present class to get over and then she shall introduce her to the coach.

Day Dreamer's Academy was a posh one. Ria noticed all age group learners coming for the classes. There were about 10 rooms for different instruments to put your hands on. It was 11.30 am and she saw a few boys coming out of the second room that faced the pantry there.

The counselor said to a man, "She is waiting there." He came and stood by her. He was tall and lean but surely had some kind of charm on his face which shone. She saw his eyes checking her out and she stood up from her seat. He introduced himself as an academy member. The man greeted her, "Hello, I am your coach, Saurav. Welcome to the academy… miss…."

Ria greeted back, "Hi coach. I am Shanaya, Shanaya Singhania."

Saurav asked, "So you are an Indian?"

Ria replied, "Indian by heart but have been brought up in Singapore."

Saurav, still checking her out, asked, "And what brings you here?"

Ria answered, "Well!! You can say the love for drums. I had always wanted to play an instrument and drums being my favorite, I thought of giving it a try. Will you please guide me to it…coach?"

A small smile played across his mouth. Saurav said, "With these looks Miss Shanaya, you shall surely go far."

Ria couldn't prevent herself from stiffening slightly at the sexist remark. Her reaction didn't escape his observant eyes.

Saurav said, "I hope I haven't offended you Miss… Shanaya."

Ria shook her head. Saurav gestured her to sit and he sat across her. He continued, "A good drummer also needs charm. So if you really want to learn the drums in a big way and make your audience love you, you need to play with all the accessories you own and not just the instrument you play."

Ria asked, "You mean.. I need to voice out while playing…."

Saurav clarified, "Nahh.. I meant you need to flaunt yourself… your looks..your body..along with the instrument." Ria bit her lip. She was all nerves.

Saurav suggested, "Don't sell yourself short. You may go a long way.. Miss Shanaya, much further than you think." His eyes saw her face and wandered down her figure. She suddenly stood up saying she needed to catch up with her aunt for lunch.

Saurav stood up too. He put his hand behind her shoulders and gestured to the door that would take her to the lucid air. Ria shivered. She tried to avoid the bombardment of sensations that started to flood her due to his touch.

Ria, making herself strong, asked, "Do you have children coach?"

Saurav replied, "Ah, my students call me coach. But you can call me Saurav, there are always exceptions.. right Shanaya? And no.. I don't have any children as I haven't yet been married." Ria wanted to leave. She could feel the evil.

Saurav held both her hands and said, "You may start your classes tomorrow. It's been long that I have had such….passion…. I mean a passionate student who wants to learn drums. I would love to make music with you.. maybe after dinner… so shall we?" Ria glanced at him. She smiled and said, "Sure, but maybe next time. I'll call you."

Saurav dreamingly said, "I am a man of intensity and passion… I'll make you go high on..…"

Ria turned quickly and without a word, she went out of the academy door to breathe….

****

Abeer saw her and yelled, "Where the hell were you?"

Ria, still trembling from the effects of Saurav's touch, walked past Abeer and sat on her bed. She wrapped the blanket around her. With shaky fingers, she started pressing her temples. Abeer looked at her. He went to her and shook her with both hands demanding an explanation about her whereabouts.

Ria scoffed, "Don't touch me. Move away."

He left her and sat beside her. Ria spoke, "I went to the academy to see Saurav."

Abeer asked shockingly, "You did.. you did what…?"

Ria said, "You wanted to be sure whether Ayaan had been kidnapped by Saurav. There was only one way to be certain. So I went to him..as a learner for drums and…."

Abeer with his hands on his forehead, "I just don't believe you! How could you go to that man when you knew how dangerous he is? Or did you go to him for your own personal reasons?"

Ria frowned and said, "Disgusting… what kind of a man are you Abeer? You think I went to him to satisfy myself? You think I am here for your money? I don't need any weapon to get things out of anyone. Just a touch will tell me everything about the person. What do you think.. how the hell did I get to know your struggles? I know you blame yourself for the loss of your mother though you were just a little boy. I know you blame no one except yourself for not giving happiness to Aarti and you also think you are at fault when Ayaan got kidnapped. Your friend Saket.. you helped him out of his depression and today he is the only one you trust in the whole world. I also know how much you hate me.. how many times you stopped yourself from touching me although you…."

And she moved her gaze from him. She had shocked him. She was on the verge of tears. She was not a person to flaunt her secret ability on her friends just to show off. But yes, to make Abeer believe in her, she would have done anything and finally she succeeded.

Ria continued, "Saurav is a jerk. But he doesn't know where Ayaan is or even about his existence. He doesn't even know where Aarti is and he doesn't care. Even if he had a child, he wouldn't have cared for him."

She had hit the nail and Abeer wondered.. Does she really know the truth or is she just playing games with him? He only believed in himself and if he had to believe her..that means he had to believe in her abilities. But no one knew about him, about how he struggled since his mother had left him. No one…except he, himself. But now she knew him. She knew everything. He just sat looking at her. With a hoarse voice, he said, "Tell me the whole story."

Ria, rubbing her skin, requested, "Later please. I want to take a hot shower now and clean that man's dirty touch on my skin." She gathered all her strength, stood up from her bed and walked straight to the bathroom. Abeer got goosebumps. He waited for Ria to come out.

Ria came out, dressed in a blue jumpsuit and asked Abeer if he could take her out for dinner as she was starving and hadn't had anything since morning. Abeer nodded and they left.

At the restaurant, she ordered hot garlic noodles, chicken fried rice, chicken red wings and some prawns. She also added a plate of baked salad with lots of leafy veggies in it. Abeer looked at her with a smile and asked, "Is this all you want?"

Ria replied, "Yes. You may select what you would like to have from the menu."

Abeer called for his dinner. He kept looking at her, wondering how a girl like her could be so daring at one time and timid at the other. While having his food, he kept looking at her from time to time. She was busy stuffing herself and didn't care about anyone around her.

Abeer inquired, "So did you inherit your vision from your mother?"

Ria looked at him with her mouth full of food.

After finishing what she had in her mouth, she answered, "No. It's my granny who has been lucky with a gift as well, though it's not exactly the same as mine."

She didn't want him to know about her granny's super predictions which had told her about Abeer's arrival nearly ten days earlier before he showed. She smiled at her secrets.

Abeer asked, "So how much is the fee that you charge for the help you provide?"

Ria answered, "Nothing. I just take the expenses incurred in the mission and nothing more than that."

Abeer questioned, "Really? Then what do you do for a living? Photography?"

Ria replied, "That's my passion and sometimes I do some freelance photography too and I also sketch."

Abeer raised his eyebrows. He thought she was trying to impress him saying she wasn't interested in money. From what he had seen in her granny's house, they weren't too well off… and she says she doesn't take fees. His interest suddenly grew in knowing her.

Abeer asked, "Don't you think you'll need to change your food habits soon? You eat like a giant."

Ria said, "Very funny." She wrinkled her nose at him. She knew if the pounds started showing, she'd have to give away all the luxuries her hunger craved for. But as for now she didn't want to bother as she was just right.

Abeer kept looking at her as she completed her food. It was a pleasure for him to see a woman enjoying her meal. He had never seen any woman eating the way Ria had. She relished every bit of her meal.

Abeer spoke, "Now that you have satisfied your hunger, please tell me about your little outing today."

Ria started, "I had no idea why you behaved so weirdly knowing the location of the motel, until yesterday night when you told me all about Saurav and Aarti. I have no idea how much time you and your Singapore police would have taken to find out whether Saurav was behind the kidnapping. So I thought of dealing with him all by myself. First I did some homework and then got myself enrolled in his academy." She then narrated all that happened with her while she was with him. Abeer listened quietly to everything she said. He then surveyed her carefully and said, "You are a detective yourself and you really want me to believe you that Saurav is not behind all this?"

Ria said, "You never trust me and I just don't know how to make you believe in me. But the truth is… I have the abilities to touch a belonging of a person and know about him. I can also get information about the person by just touching him."

Abeer asked with curiosity, "And how does that work?"

Ria replied, "Well… sometimes I can shield myself but I can't always control it."

Abeer asked, "So you touched him… and that helped you get information out of him?"

Ria said, "I did go thinking I would touch him. But he touched me. He held me tight and ….." she started breathing fast.

Abeer asked, "And what? Did he hurt you? Tell me…"

Ria said, "His touch told me everything about him. But I felt suffocated by his grip. He is a jerk and a womanizer. He is evil.. I saw him with a knife…"

Abeer saw her shivering and took her back to the hotel room. He thought of carrying her as she started losing her colour. But then.. he was scared of making her jump.

She sat on the bed and covered herself with a blanket.

Abeer inquired, "Are you fine?" She nodded. He sat beside her.

Abeer said, "You said he had a knife in his hand… why? What more did you see?"

Ria said, "I saw him killing a man.. his face was not visible to me but I know he killed him."

Abeer was shocked. He believed her. He told her, "I am flying back tomorrow and you are coming along."

Ria said, "You can carry on. I'll do what I want to."

Abeer said, "That man is dangerous. He'll trace you."

Ria ignored his statement, "Have you chosen what you want?"

Abeer said, "Yes."

Ria asked, "What?"

Abeer replied, "I'll stay back…..for you." He smiled and left the room.

****

Ria lay awake. All she could think of was Abeer. Why did he stay back for her? Did she hear it wrong? She got up and went to get Ayaan's toy out of her bag. As soon as she touched it, colours flashed in front of her and she dropped the toy on the floor. She was scared to pick it up. What if Ayaan is dead.. how will she face Abeer and Aarti. What will she tell them? No. Ayaan has to be alive.. for his mother.. and specially for Abeer.

Many times, she had witnessed horrible and heart breaking visions. She was still terrified. But then it's always better to know the truth than worrying about it when you know you have the abilities to face it. She tied her hair in a tight bun and had a glass of water. Without wasting a second more, she picked the toy from the floor.

She waited for the visions of the little boy who loved this toy to come … and she started getting weak.. 'She saw him sitting in a pool of sand.. on a beach.. he was throwing sand on himself.. and then a man came and pulled him by his hand… and the little boy started crying…' Ria started shivering. She hurriedly opened her eyes and ran for the bed and once again passed out.

Abeer came to her room and saw her lay still. He checked her breathing cycle and then covered her with a blanket and waited for her to come back to her senses. After a long wait, Ria flung her eyes open. She saw Abeer staring at her and told him to take out a pill from her bag. He obeyed her immediately. She tried to pick the tablet from his palm without touching him. Pushing the tablet and the glass of water down her throat, she again slept. Abeer waited patiently for her to wake up. He picked the toy that Ria had used to find out about Ayaan.

Ria woke up and saw Abeer with Ayaan's toy. She sat straight on her bed. Her temples were still paining and her eyes were burning. Ria spoke, "He is somewhere near the sea."

Abeer asked, "And now we need to hunt the beaches here?"

Ria nodded, "Yes…" Abeer stared at her. She continued, "My instinct will lead us to him. Let's go. We need to hurry before we

lose him."

They got into the rented car and drove off. Abeer kept driving where Ria's instinct told her to.

Abeer asked, "So do you like living with your granny? Do you have friends up there? Have you ever dated?" He wanted to know everything about her.

Ria replied, "Let's make a deal Abeer. For every question I answer of yours, you too shall answer mine, without a lie."

And they chatted like two good friends asking each other all about their lives and answering honestly to each other.

Ria seemed to go to great lengths to avoid touching people. He started noticing her more and tried not to offend her by any of his taunting remarks or touches. He remembered the times she couldn't avoid his touches and it took her hours to recover from the pain due to it. He wondered how she would react if she ever went through an intimate touch.….with him. A picture of Ria started forming in his mind. He glanced at her. She was lounging next to him, with her feet up on the dashboard in front of her. He returned his attention on the road. She was nothing but a help to search for Ayaan. He wanted nothing more from her. Nothing.….. ********

The darkness grew deep and she went back to her room, to the hotel.

****

Abeer shut his eyes in pain. He thought about Ayaan and Aarti.

Chapter 5

♡

"Stop yelling at me… it was you who wanted to drive and drive and drive… I had told you a few hours back to stop and rest. But the great ABEER SINGH only listens to himself. The stubborn man."

Abeer reverted back, "At least be thankful we found a decent place to halt the car in such a deserted area."

She made a face at him which was barely visible in the dark of the night. Somehow, without tripping, they managed their way to an aloof house. It was dark. Ria took out a torch and flashed it on, to see what the place looked like. Abeer went inside followed by her. It looked clean. She seemed glad they had a roof above them.

Ria exclaimed, "Wow. This is heaven. I am so tired.. just the right time for me to doze off. By the way, where are you camping tonight?"

Abeer replied, "Well.. I am gonna be close by… right beside you."

Ria looked at him. Her heart started beating fast. "You mean you are staying here… in this house..here..with me.. no..no..not possible..you kidding…."

Abeer found a corner and went and sat there. "Is it okay if I stay here tonight?"

Ria biting her lips, "Yes of course. Why should I have any problem?"

She wanted to run away, sharing the same roof with Abeer gave her goosebumps. She saw him opening his bag and taking out his nightwear, his shaving kit, all that he required. She wondered how he could be so calm while she was in the room.

She knew he didn't like her much. It was going to be hard having him around. She moved to her bag and took out her nightgown. She walked towards the bathroom and locked the door.

She took a shower and came out, all set to rush to the bed without even taking a look at him. She saw him and froze. She saw him unbuttoning his shirt. He saw her and casually said, "If you are done with the bathroom, I too would like to freshen up."

She looked at him. She wanted to reply back but suddenly couldn't get any words out. Her eyes went immediately to his bare chest. She stopped breathing. He crossed her. Suddenly he came back to her and asked, "What happened? All fine?"

Ria asked, "What do you want from me?"

Abeer whispered, "What I want from you? What I want is what I have always wanted. I want to get to the end of this. I want… Ayaan."

She suddenly came back to her senses and realized Abeer had started believing in her abilities. But his smell started making her weak. Both of them felt a silent invitation to explore the other. Abeer was checking her out. She had no make–up on her face. The nightgown she wore was quite decent but the satin material made it impossible to hide the fact that she wasn't wearing a bra.

Abeer asked in a husky voice, "Do you want to know what more I want from you?"

Ria looked at him and he could see her face was calm and easily readable. He inhaled the smell of her wet shampooed hair. Moving back a little, he said, "I want you to tell me something Ria."

He saw her biting her lips repeatedly. Abeer said in a low voice, "Tell me what happens to you when you touch me?"

She lowered her eyes. He waited for her to answer but she had no answer. He smiled as he knew what she felt, though she did not utter a word.

Abeer continued, "Let me tell you what happens to me. Little currents of electricity pass under my skin everytime I touch you. I am sure you feel it too. Yes Ria?"

She was happy, very happy to know he felt the same for her. She knew this but wasn't sure. But she had to control her thoughts. She stared at him.

Abeer said, "I know you felt the sparks too. I know it all started up the hill when I first touched you. But why are you so scared of me?" Ria said, "I am not scared of anyone."

Abeer said in a husky voice, "I think you are. You are still afraid of me. Is it because of the reaction you have never felt before or do I look scary? Tell me Ria. Please."

His mouth went close to hers. How she longed for this! She wanted to touch his lips…wanted to feel them..wanted to taste them… Her senses were overtaken by this man's responses.

He whispered in her ears, "I want you to admit it. Be honest to me."

Her eyes shut as he dropped a kiss on her lips. She shivered.

Abeer asked, "Do you react the same way when anyone touches you?"

Ria replied, "No." She looked at him. She could read him now.

Abeer whispered, "Touch me now Ria." She shook her head.

His lips went to her cheeks, her ears, her chin and deep down her neck. The desire for him started making her weak down her knees. She turned and wanted to get away but his lips followed hers. She felt flutters of desire down her veins. He had never been this close to her. No one had ever kissed her or made her crave. His hands touched her face.. his thumb started making way to her lips. His lips pressed hers, making her lips go apart. She tasted the desire in him. His body warmed hers. He lost his control and kissed her harder. She knew he wasn't pretending. She couldn't ignore his real desire for her. Going on her toes, she kissed him back. The first taste of her response made Abeer go crazy and his kiss hardened. Ria also responded the same way. His fingers slowly started moving to her cleavage and she could feel her nipples getting tight. His one hand didn't leave her face while the other cupped her left breast. His kiss was making her go mad. She wanted to melt in his arms. He drew her hands around his neck. He then pressed her closer until she was trapped between the walls and his bare chest. Her skin felt unbearably hot against his. He seemed reluctant to let her go. She felt the sweet reality of wanting, by this man. He tightened his grip. He wanted her. His fingers rubbed her skin with slow sensual touches. And then… she saw the flashes… though the flashes were not the usual ones…she pushed him back fiercely. He left her and stepped back. She ran to her bed and turned towards the other side. The flashes showed her… the love..the hunger that both had for each other… under the silk black covers… and her face turned red.

He went to the bathroom and she could hear the sound of the shower. He came out and saw her sleeping or maybe pretending to be fast asleep. He went to his corner and kept thinking of her. He kept looking at the ceiling. Sleep was miles away from him. He kept imagining her. The restless night was soon gone with the rays of the rising sun.

The next morning she avoided looking at him. But he was perfectly fine. Though they were not talkative, she could sense he had again filled himself with attitude towards her. They drove and drove to the parts of the country which Ria's intuitions told her. She started shivering. He saw her sinking in the seat beside her and asked, "Are you cold? Are you sick?"

Ria answered, "No. I am fine." For the first time he felt stupid. How could he get evoked by this lady? She had no feelings for him and he took the initiative yesterday. He was angry at himself. He thought he had offended her by kissing her yesterday…or by any of his moves? He knew there was something between them and he still longed for it. The thoughts kept coming to him. He should have never touched her, because now it was impossible for him to forget the feel of her and her taste. He saw her shivering and stopped the car. He got down and opened his bag to get a sweater out of her bag and gave it to her. He was really worried as it wasn't cold enough to put a sweater on her. He asked, "Are you sure you're fine?"

Ria, still shivering under the warm sweater, "The closer we get to Ayaan, I'll get more cold. Keep driving. Don't stop. We are not far." Abeer started driving again. Ria kept directing him and suddenly they started nearing a beach. He stopped the car and Ria stepped out. Abeer was really concerned about her health but she took speed. He followed her. She kept walking….crossed the beach…and came to an ice-cream shop.

Abeer was irritated and yelled at her, "Now you want to have an ice-cream? Do you have any idea about your health? It seems you have caught the flu. Come on. Let's get back to the car. He is not here."

But Ria didn't listen to him and walked inside the ice-cream parlor. She looked around and in a corner by the window.. it was there.. she pointed to Abeer. He felt his feet taking him to the corner where Ria pointed. He bent down and picked up a light blue coloured romper. The color had faded out of it. He turned towards Ria. Abeer immediately went to the ice cream counter and asked the man on the other side if he could make a few calls. Abeer first called Saket and told him everything that happened. Saket was glad to hear about the lead. He suggested Abeer to call the Singapore police and hand them the case now. After another five minutes of discussion, Abeer hung up the receiver. He then made another call and this time it was to the cop who was assigned Ayaan's case in Singapore. He narrated the whole scene to him. He told him about the romper, about the place where he found it and that the romper cannot be of anybody else other than Ayaan. He was wearing it on the day he was kidnapped. The cop found it silly and said it was a mere coincidence as the romper must have been manufactured in millions and just by picking up one from an ice-cream parlor, he cannot go on the search for the kid. The lead doesn't work this way. Abeer hung up furiously.

Ria was still cold and shivering. She wanted to get away from the place but not without knowing about Ayaan's case. She looked at him. He quietly went and sat at a table. He held the romper very close to him and she could see tears running down his cheeks. Gathering all the strength, she walked to him. Her heart ached for him. She could not believe he is the same Abeer who was so strong and confident just a couple of seconds back. She dropped to her knees in front of him. He didn't look at her but knew she was there.

He voiced out, "Aarti was just three when our mother left us. She was all that I had. I had promised myself to look after her and never let her know about poverty or loneliness. She was my strength and I made sure she got the best. I didn't want her to learn how ugly the life could be without parents. My father was an abusive man. He was never loyal to my mother. He didn't even look after us after she departed and one day we found him dead on the roads. A car had crushed him. Later we found out he was hit by someone who was once his partner. My grandfather had left enough money for both of us to live on. We were sent to a children's home where we were brought up for eight years and then the court decided to let us be on our own."

Ria always wanted him to throw away his mask. But seeing him broken was not what she wished for. He cried, "I have failed her. She'll never trust me again."

Ria said, "It doesn't matter what the cop thinks. Believe me, for once, Ayaan was there on the beach. He was here at this icecream parlor. I know you don't trust me…"

Abeer looked up at her, "I believe you. I am not a man to whom faith comes easily, but I have faith in you." She looked at him. She knew he was honest.

Abeer said, "I can't fail this time. I have to have Ayaan alive for my sister Aarti."

Ria pacified him, "Ayaan is alive Abeer. You won't fail. We will get him back, no matter what. Aarti will have him. The boy will be back soon. I promise you. I won't let you fail."

They went back to the hotel. Ria got him a cup of coffee but he was in no mood to sip it. She touched his hand to make him feel she is with him and they'll get Ayaan back together.

He felt her soft hands on his shoulders and the electric current yet again passed between them. Before she could move her hands, he caught them and held them tightly. He stood up and faced her. Their lips were close to each other.

Abeer spoke, "You are the only hope I have in finding Ayaan and I don't want to lose this hope."

Ria nodded and gazed at him. He looked into her eyes. She could see the desire that she had once seen in the deserted house.

Ria requested, "Please let me go."

He shook his head and whispered in her ears, "Please."

She knew how desperately he wanted her. She knew how desperately she wanted him.

And she knew… the fears… She had to stop him… and she will stop him.

FINDING AYAAN

Chapter 6

Abeer kneeled down as if begging her not to run away from him and pulled her down. She, with shaky hands tried to shoo him off but his grip was too strong on her. He didn't let her go. His mouth went immediately to her throat and she gasped. More than anything else he wanted to lose himself in her. He knew her skin burned when it touched his, the same way his did when it came in contact with hers. Fire was the word. Current passed in their skin wherever they touched… he ached for her… He could see her breathe insanely. He tongued her neck. He recognized the emotions because he too had similar ones. Ria shivered. There was no fear. There were no visions. His touch stripped her of all illusions. She could not pretend any more and she loosened herself to him. Her lips parted naturally as his mouth covered hers. She knew this taste and it made her go wild. Her fingers dug into his skin. The passion flowed to her. Her stomach felt thousands of triggers in it. She was thirsty for him. Their tongues mated. He touched both her breasts. He could feel the nipples getting erect even under her clothes. He teased them. The pleasure made her desire come alive. Now there was no looking back. She felt his strong hands on her back. He made her lie on the carpeted floor slowly. He kissed her as he leaned on her. She gasped. He drowned her with kisses all over her face…he bit her ears and she moaned. He slowly fingered her neckline not leaving an inch without a kiss. Her legs parted and he pressed himself against her. His kiss on her lips was more fierce. They kissed breathlessly. His hands went to her top and he pulled it out from where it had been tucked. His hands went under the top and made their way to her breasts which were still covered by her bra.

He cupped them. She could feel the excitement in her body. But she feared…

"Let me go", she pleaded. And he moved away from her.

Ria looked down, "Please leave now."

Abeer said, "Not unless you tell me."

Ria spoke, "There's nothing to say. I need rest. Leave me alone."

Abeer said, "That's not possible anymore."

Ria looked at him. He didn't blink once and kept staring at her.

Abeer asked, "Tell me, why are you so scared? I know I am new to you but even you are new to me." He examined her profile. He knew the urge to make her, his, was killing him inside.

Ria hesitantly, "I don't have much experience."

Abeer, still eyeing her, "That's not possible. I am sure men would have drooled over you. You are beautiful Ria."

Ria, biting her lips, "I have dated a few… but… I could never… you know how visions come to me when I get touched… so.. I never… okay… I am still a Virgin."

Abeer said, "Ohh.. your visions.. how could I forget them? Is this the reason for you to shrug me back? Do you feel the same flashes when I touch you?"

Ria with great confidence whispered, "No. It's different."

Abeer came and sat beside her. He was glad she didn't have any painful visions when they touched each other. He touched her silky hair and untied it.

Abeer spoke, "You can't deny the fact Ria. There is something between us. We both are crazily attracted to each other. Both of us have a real desire for each other. You can't run away from this. I promise you.. once we get Ayaan back, we shall finish it off."

He stood up and left her room. She too stood up and went to her bed and cried her heart out. She knew… yes… she has been trapped and now…nothing can happen.. she was in love. She has fallen in love with Abeer. But he said he'll be finishing it off.

The sun rays hit her face and slowly she opened her eyes. She saw Abeer sitting on a chair across her bed and she sat up immediately. She was thrilled to see Abeer had got her breakfast in the room. She threw her blanket and without wasting a second, she went to the beautifully laid breakfast and started crushing the food in her mouth.

Abeer kept looking at her. He found her more beautiful today. Her strappy nighty was calling him but he controlled himself as he didn't want her to get offended again. Ria saw him checking her out but she was relaxed. She was happy thinking about the little lovey dovey scene they had last night. She now knew this man had no control over himself when it came to her but then that's the way she too felt.

Abeer kept looking at her eating. He felt happy and fresh. She completed her breakfast and rushed to the bathroom to take a quick shower as they were running late. She told him they needed to go to the amusement park which was about eleven hours drive from where they were stationed. He immediately picked up the telephone and made the arrangements.

She found herself sitting beside him in a private jet that he had rented. He knew she'll be struggling again but then they had no choice. They had to get Ayaan before they again lose him and flying would make the hours of waiting easier for them. He saw her face. It was pale. She started sweating. He held her hands. She wanted to shrug him off but then it calmed her down. There were no visions at all. She stared at him. Their eyes met. He wanted her as strongly as she wanted him. She then rested her head on the seat. She knew this was their last journey together. Once Ayaan was found, everything would be finished between them. ********

They drove to the nearest hotel that was linked to the amusement park.

It was dark by the time they came back to the hotel from the park. They couldn't cover the area as it was too huge. They knew they'll have to start the search again tomorrow. Ria was exhausted. Abeer ordered dinner and they both ate silently. He could see her face getting pale and she was too weak. He helped her into the bed and walked back to his room. Sleep came to Ria within a second. He too went to bed thinking about her. It scared him to accept the fact that he was getting possessive about her. He wanted to shield her from the world. Thinking the same, he dozed off.

The next morning was a beautiful one. They both woke up energized and got ready. Abeer came to her room with breakfast and without a word they both completed it. Ria surveyed him. His gaze went to hers. She said, "Let's go and get Ayaan home."

The park was filled with characters. There were hundreds of people. Kids were running all over the park. Rides were on. Ria started feeling cold. Abeer kept scanning the crowd. He made sure no one came near Ria. She was amazed by his flawless concern. They both kept walking without a word. Abeer saw her shaking and asked her if she wanted something.

Ria said, "Abeer, he is here."

Abeer looked at her and she gestured with her hand to her right. Abeer told her to wait there but she didn't listen. She shivered and holding Abeer's hands, they both ran to the place that her intuition told her. They looked around. He saw her taking out Ayaan's toy from her handbag. Visions started at once. Her face became pale and she shivered breathlessly. She opened her eyes and started walking. Abeer followed her. They had to find him. Suddenly she stopped and turned to her left. She wanted to speak up. Her lips were shaking. She took a deep breath. Her legs went weak. Her hands were heavy. She at once saw him. Yes.. it was him. No, she can't pass out now. She has to get him. She held the fence near her and turned towards Abeer. But he was nowhere. She again looked at the crowd where she had spotted him.. but now where was he? She can't lose him. Forcing her legs to move, she started pushing the people who faced her… and then she again saw him. She saw Ayaan.

Taking a deep breath and with lots of courage, she started walking into the crowd.

Abeer was checking all the toddlers he crossed while going against the crowd. He didn't care if anyone was rude to him. He kept pushing people to see the kids in the strollers. He didn't want to miss even one. He had to find him and this was his only chance.

But suddenly he realized Ria was not with him. Where was she? He called her name loudly several times, but she was nowhere. He started his way back from where they both had started. He can't let her get hurt. He had to be with her. He pushed through the people and he saw her sitting on her knees holding a stroller tightly with her fingers. He rushed to her.

The stroller… he recognized it. He peeped inside it and there he saw… Ayaan… he saw the boy fiddling with Ria's hair.

The woman with the stroller warned Ria, "Move back, else I'll call the police."

Abeer spoke, "That's what we are waiting for. I'll help you."

Abeer took the charge and he held her forearm tightly. She jerked but couldn't free herself.

Abeer screamed loudly, "Security. Someone get the security."

He suddenly looked at Ria. She still had a strong grip on the stroller. He gave her a concerned look. The woman took a chance and freed herself. She turned and ran a few steps but was again caught by Abeer. By this time the security had come and they took her by her elbow. He walked back to the stroller and Ria. He looked at Ayaan. It was a dream to him. He had found him. He just couldn't believe it. Ayaan was right in front of him. He touched his cheeks and Ayaan looked up.

Abeer lovingly spoke to Ayaan, "Hey dude…. How are you? Did you miss me?"

Ayaan smiled at him. He knew the face. He knew him. He released the hold he had on Ria's hair and started clapping. His face shone. He was happy. He was excited.

Abeer took his nephew in his arms. He hugged him tightly and kissed him all over his chubby cheeks. This was still a dream to him. He just couldn't believe he had Ayaan in his arms. This was a miracle for him. He looked at the sky and felt grateful for the first time in his life. So many times he had dreamt of having Ayaan back in his life but somewhere down he had started losing the hope. And today.. Ayaan was in his arms. He hugged him again tightly.

"You need to come with us. Give us the boy," the head security told him. Abeer willingly gave Ayaan to him. He then looked at Ria. She was lying still. He bent down to her, "Ria, open your eyes." But there was no response. He asked the crowd to leave the place and slowly they started departing. He told the security that he shall not leave without her. He kneeled down to her and took her hands in his and started rubbing them. He felt guilty for her present state. He should have never left her side. But the damage was done. He started panicking. He didn't know what to do to make her feel better. He wanted her to open her eyes. He wanted her to talk to him. But she didn't move.

And after many long minutes, she opened her eyes.

Ria whispered, "Abeer…."

Abeer smiled, "Yes Ria. I am here. I am here, right beside you darling."

She slowly started coming back. He helped her stand on her feet. Ria is filled with fear.

She looked at Abeer and inquired, "Ayaan?"

Abeer with a smile, "He is fine. You found him darling."

She smiled at him. She lost her control and fainted. He carried her in his arms and went with the security to his nephew. He told them to call the police as he wanted to speak to them straight. The police came and asked Abeer how he traced the kidnappers. They wanted him to come down to the police station to complete the formalities. But as Abeer had high contacts, they released him with Ria and Ayaan and told him to meet them once everything was stable.

Abeer looked at Ria, who was lying on the sofa. The cops handed Ayaan to him. Ayaan was delighted and so was Abeer. The security there helped him into a car with both Ria and Ayaan. Abeer took the stroller and Ria's bag too with him. He was glad that finally the mission was over and Ayaan was with him.

Chapter 7

While leaving from the park, he told the cops to inform him what the lady who had kidnapped Ayaan told them. He shall see to it that she is not spared. Abeer also told them that the woman was not alone and he thinks there is a man too who had teamed up with her. The cops promised to call Abeer as soon as they finished questioning the lady. The cops nodded and Abeer along with his precious gift and Ria left for the hotel.

Back at the hotel room, Abeer made Ria comfortable on her bed. She was exhausted. Her eyes were shut and she had a calm expression on her face. She was still holding Abeer's hands tightly and it was difficult to loosen her grip. Slowly Abeer moved her fingers off him and covered her with a blanket. He then turned towards Ayaan who was rolling on the carpet happily. He bent down and picked him up in his arms.

"Abee Abee…" Ayaan started as Abeer carried him on his shoulders. He had his sister's most precious asset with him. He was the happiest man on this earth today and he knew it was Ria who got him this happiness.

He went to his room and called Aarti. She smiled. She knew Ria fulfilled her promise. Abeer had her Ayaan with him and he was safe. Ayaan… he was back. Abeer then conversed with Saket for a while. He hung up the phone and ordered a glass of milk for Ayaan.

Ayaan was not left alone for a second. He waited for him to sleep and then carried him in his arms to check if Ria woke up. But she was still sleeping and he didn't have a heart to wake her up at this hour. He shut the door again and went to his room with Ayaan.

Saket and Abeer hugged each other as they saw Aarti tightly holding Ayaan in her arms. She just couldn't resist the happy tears flowing down her cheeks, from her eyes. Sheela too hugged her and made sure Aarti took a good rest as she was still weak.

Abeer said, "Good you guys came up here. It's such a delight to see the boy in his mother's arms."

Saket said, "None of us could waste a second to see him again. It was your good work that we have Ayaan back."

Abeer corrected him, "Ria. She did everything. I was only following her instructions and that too half heartedly. If it wasn't her, the bunch of happiness wouldn't have been ours today. We owe her everything."

Suddenly he remembered her. He had got a doctor for her to inject the sedative so that she could get a good peaceful nap. He had also piled a couple of blankets on her as he knew the shivering would last a good eight hours for her.

Saket patted him on his shoulders. He surveyed him. "Hope all is fine. We all need to leave for the airport in another 20 minutes. I have made all travel arrangements and we shall be in Mumbai by late evening today."

Abeer spoke, "Great. Make sure she is safe. Get all our security men to the house. I want both of them to be safe. Once I am back I'll take the charge. You are the only one I can trust."

Saket, staring at him, "You are not coming with us? Why?"

Abeer shook his head. "Ah well.. I need to meet the cops. I want to get each and every information out of that lady. The man who is still roaming free can again be a threat to us. I need to finish it off….."

Saket inquired, "And how long will you be staying here?"

Abeer answered, "I need to deal with the police. I can't give that man another chance. It can be a week or maybe two. Please keep yourself armed." Saket assured him saying he shall guard them day and night. Abeer nooded with a smile.

Aarti was really disturbed as she couldn't thank Ria herself. She was still sleeping. Abeer told her he shall make them talk on the phone once she wakes up. Aarti didn't want to leave Abeer. But then it was time to go back. Abeer got Ayaan's favorite toy out of Ria's bag and gave it to him. He was delighted to have it. He then hugged both Aarti and Ayaan and they all left for the airport.

He re-entered her room. She was still sleeping. He walked over to her bed and gazed at her. Her breathing was still deep. With a gentle hand, he pushed her silky hair off her face. He then pulled a chair right in front of her bed and rested himself in it. The night seemed long but it was still and calm. The room was quiet. She opened her eyes and removed the heap of blankets off her. She slowly sat up. Her memories filtered back to her. All she could remember was… Ayaan. She had found him. They had found him. Her head felt as if a bell was hitting it but still the memories were not clear. She had blurred visions after she found Ayaan and she frowned. The bright sunlight spilled the hot rays through the curtains into her room. She slipped out of her bed, paused to switch on the air-conditioner and then headed straight to the bathroom. Standing under the shower, Ria started feeling human again. Her head was throbbing. She washed her hair and then went still, as the memory of being undressed completely by Abeer and lying under a blanket kept piercing in her mind. She took a deep breath and pushed the thought away. And then her hands started shaking as she remembered being touched with dozens of strangers. Their worries, phobias and desires… started filling her head. She started getting weak. She filtered her thoughts and again the blissful memory of having Ayaan back came to her. She felt happy thinking about the little boy. He was safe and now he was back. And this means… her usefulness to Abeer had come to an end. She was overjoyed with the fact that Ayaan was finally back but her heart ached as it knew she was heading towards the end of her journey with Abeer.

Coming out of the shower, she wrapped herself with a towel and grabbed another one for her wet hair. She walked back to the bedroom and at once sensed his presence in her room.

She froze. Abeer was standing silently in a corner of her room. She forgot what she was draped with and the towel that she had grabbed to dry her wet hair slipped from her hands and fell on the floor. He suddenly turned around to face her. She held her wrapped towel with both hands to secure the desire that was burning behind it.

Without taking his eyes from her, he drew the curtains. He looked at her from head to toe. She looked fragile. The sight of her in the towel provoked him. He came closer to her and touched her cheeks with his thumb. He then bent down and picked up the other towel that had been lying on the carpeted floor. He went behind her and started drying her wet hair with the towel. She remained frozen. Her mind wanted to act but her feet were stuck to the ground. She didn't move an inch. Suddenly she felt his deep breaths from behind. She turned to face him. He held her shoulders with both his hands and shut his eyes. Ria jerked to free herself. He watched her with heavy eyes. She skipped a heart-beat as she realized he had been thinking about her under the black satin. Her mouth went dry and she started biting her lips. He was half hungry and half dangerous.

With shaky lips, she said, "Abeer. I need to get dressed."

Abeer stepped back. He could still smell her fragrance. The man inside him wanted to hold her.. kiss her wildly.. but he controlled his emotions. Abeer said, "I brought you something to wear" and gestured to the chair. She noticed a dress on it.

Ria spoke, "I have clothes Abeer."

Abeer said, "Yes….but I wanted you to wear this. I am taking you out."

Ria questioned, "Where? And Why?"

Abeer said, "Aren't you hungry? While you were asleep for the past 32 hours, I went around and got both of us booked for dinner at a fine restaurant. You will really like it."

Ria, shocked, "32 hours? That's way ahead… I have never slept more than 12 hours at a stretch."

Abeer said, "I don't think you have ever been touched by a huge crowd and that too within a minute. You have never experienced such trauma earlier. Do you think I don't know what you felt when you found Ayaan in that crowd? Why the hell did you allow such pain to yourself Ria? I told you to stay away from the crowd."

Ria, looking into his eyes, "I had to go… I knew it would be difficult for you to hunt him in such a big crowd. I knew I could find him. I had to find him for…"

He saw her shaking again and cursed himself for starting the conversation. Picking the soft silky strand of her hair, he started rubbing it between his thumb and index finger. He then started winding it between his two fingers.

Abeer said, "I know I have never trusted you and have been too rude to you many times, but I am not ungrateful. I owe you everything. If it wasn't you, we would have never found Ayaan."

Their eyes met. She dropped her gaze from the intense look of his. Abeer said, "I don't know how much pain you caused to yourself with it. But I know what you were like when everything was over."

Ria was listening to each and every word of his but she didn't have the courage to face him. She felt weak.

Abeer said, "I really don't understand. Why do you need to do this to yourself? Why do you need to hurt yourself and that too for strangers?"

The word strangers hit her. Her mind started talking to her. How could he even think they were strangers! They have touched each other. They have seen desire in each other's eyes. She knew he wanted her as desperately as she wanted him. But, strangers… is that what they both are? Is that all?

Ria made him understand, "What's the use of my gift if I can't help others? But then it's not always so bad… it's only a…"

Abeer interrupted, "Yeah right. Every time you get visions, you take pain relief tablets. You shiver. You get pale. Many times I have seen you passing out too. You get weak. And here you are telling me.. it's not always so bad."

She smiled seeing his concern and said, "I am helping people because I choose to do so. It gives me happiness too. I feel a great amount of satisfaction within myself."

But he wasn't convinced. He wanted to shield her. What if someday someone took advantage of her priceless gift? World is ugly and she is too innocent for it. He couldn't let her get hurt. It was his duty to guard her from the world. She was aware of others' needs but never of hers. She could relate to others emotions by touching them but then what about her emotions…

Suddenly moving away from his thoughts, he let her hair free from his fingers and stepped back. The thought of protecting her was not the first time that lingered in his mind. She was nothing for him except a help in the mission. The mission was over. Ayaan was back. And now..nothing more mattered.

Ria asked, "Where is Ayaan? I want to see him."

Abeer replied, "He left with Aarti, Saket and Sheela. They were here yesterday. Aarti really wanted to meet you and thank you. But then I didn't let her as you were on rest. She was upset. But I promised her to make you speak to her soon. They all flew back to Mumbai. You may speak to her tomorrow."

Ria inquired, "Hmm.. and what about the kidnapper? Did she spill out anything?"

Abeer said, "Ria….."

Ria, "Yes?"

Abeer asked, "Do you still want to continue chatting with that towel draped on you?" Ria could feel the heat getting into her again.

Abeer said, "Because if you like it this way, I don't know how much longer you'll have it on you." She started getting weak on her knees. His words echoed.

Abeer said, "Get dressed. I'll be back soon."

He went out of the door leaving her breathless. She fell on her bed and shut her eyes.

Ria had read the look he had worn. She was inexperienced. But Abeer was surely a practiced lover. He had the ability to satisfy any woman. She sat on the edge of the bed. She really didn't know what a virgin woman of her age would do to satisfy his needs.

****

He ordered a bottle of wine along with the food. The waiter took the order and left.

Abeer turned his attention to Ria. She was looking beautiful. Her face was calm and he hoped the food would make her feel good too. She had tied her hair in a bun which he didn't like. He wanted to tumble her soft silky hair over her shoulders and down her back. He had fantasized having it spread over his chest many times. His fingers were itching for a touch of it. The thought made his eyes heavy. Her appearance was killing him.

He had chosen a perfect dress for her. It highlighted her skin colour. The dress draped her curves perfectly. The straps on her shoulders were thin giving her flesh a bare look. He gazed at her cleavage which gave a perfect way to her breasts. The dress was several inches above her knees.

Every man in the dining area was gawking at her. He didn't like it and had a severe urge to take her back to the hotel… to his room. But he sat still and kept looking at her.

Ria inquired, "What's wrong Abeer? Are you okay?"

Abeer's thoughts were broken, "Huh… uh.. yes.. am fine." He tried looking calm, though he was fully aroused by her thoughts.

Ria asked, "Alright. Hey… you didn't tell me about the woman we got arrested. Did she say anything?"

Abeer replied, "She hasn't opened her mouth yet. All we know is that her name is Ramya. I shall be meeting her tomorrow."

Ria offered, "I can help too."

Abeer said sternly, "No, that's not needed. I know you want to help but I can manage. You will not come with me and I shall not let you touch her under any circumstances."

Ria said irritatedly, "You can't force your decisions on me."

He tried to calm her down. "Ria, you need rest. Your body and mind need to relax. The intensity you went through at the park wasn't the usual one for you. So you have to listen to me and take good care of yourself. I can manage this alone."

Ria said angrily, "Let's see."

He looked at her and knew there was no point making her understand. She could never shield herself and was ready to do anything for anyone.

The waiter got the bottle of wine and poured some in the two wine glasses on the table. He placed the glasses in front of Ria and Abeer and excused himself.

Ria said, "I don't drink."

Abeer insisted, "Just one glass of wine won't do any harm."

She took a sip. He smiled at her. He knew she wouldn't have another glass so there was nothing to worry. But she surprised him with three glasses of wine down her throat. He stared at her lips. The wine had moistened her lips. He imagined himself licking the moisture from her soft sweet lips.

The food arrived and both of them started having it without a word. Ria kept stealing glances of him while he was busy relishing the food on his platter. The black suit and white shirt that he wore, suited him perfectly. She had never thought of him more than anything but a client. But today he was a lot more to her. She knew the flame that sprang between them. His touch made her forget herself. It was totally new to her and she was glad that it was him, she gave her authority to. He was the man who evoked her and she knew.. very soon he'll vanish from her life. ********

Ria pleaded, "I am not a tipsy dude. I can walk. Stop holding me. I want to go out. I am still not tired. Please… please let's go for a drive."

He looked at her and smiled. She might not be tipsy but the amount of wine she had was incredible for a first timer. The colour of her cheeks had changed with the intake of the wine and so he got her back to the hotel. They could have gone for a drive or something, but he didn't want to risk it. She protested but his grip was firm on her till they reached the hotel floor.

He changed the topic so that he could distract her.

Abeer said, "I know we could have gone out but then I need to go to the police station tomorrow to check with Ramya. I also need to finish a few formalities."

Ria said, "But wouldn't the cops call you if she says anything about the kidnapping?"

Abeer said, "I hope she does. But she is keeping mum, so I want to speak to her myself on this. I want to give it a try."

Ria noticed Abeer removing his coat and putting it on the chair of his room. He then unbuttoned the top two buttons of his shirt too. He removed his shoes. Seeing him this way, Ria's mouth went dry. He looked so seductive. It seemed as if he was strip-teasing her. She could see the black curls on his chest, though he was still well covered. He then unbuttoned his cuffs. He sensed Ria gazing at him and looked at her.

He went to her and asked, "What's wrong with you? Are you not feeling fine?"

She was still. She said nothing and kept gazing at him.

Abeer called loudly, "Ria…."

She came back to her senses. He examined her. He noted the way her gaze kept slipping from his and then returned back. Masculine satisfaction made him smile at her. He surveyed her. She was still gazing at him. He went up to her.

Abeer asked, "Are you sure you're alright Ria?"

She started biting her upper lip and shook her head dumbly. Her mind told her to leave..but her feet were stuck to the floor. She didn't move an inch and stared at him

Abeer, with his finger, traced down her throat…her pulse was racing. He could feel her shiver, as his thumb touched her cheeks. He wanted her to look at him but her eyes were heavy and she was looking at the floor. He lifted her chin and she shut her eyes. She didn't want to make the mistake of looking at him now. He came closer to her and she could feel his breath near her right ear.

Abeer spoke, "Now you don't even want to look at me.. did I do anything to offend you?"

Then she made the mistake of looking in his eyes…. And all she could see was desire. Their eyes remained locked. He took all the liberties. He fingered her shoulders following the thin straps of her dress. He then moved his fingers to the neckline of her dress. She gasped. Her breathing became super fast as Abeer moved his fingers to her breasts. He circled them gracefully. He then dipped one of his fingers into the exposed cleavage and she couldn't breathe. He cupped her shoulders. There were sparks flowing between them.

Abeer, in a husky voice, "There are thousands of fireworks that I can feel…beneath my hands, everytime I touch you Ria. Don't you feel the same? Tell me. That's how you felt up on the hills the day I met you for the first time.. on that rock when I touched you. That's why you moved away from me." She trembled.

He bent his head a little to her shoulders and took deep breaths making her shiver. He then touched her bare shoulders and she suddenly turned around to face him.

Abeer said, "I am still waiting for you to answer me."

Ria whispered, "Yes." She saw a satisfied smile on his face. He slipped his hands slowly from her shoulders to her palms…touching each and every inch of her hands. She was scared. She was waiting for the visions to come again to her but nothing came. The sensations caused by his touch were far too strong to get her distracted by any visions.

Abeer in a commanding voice to Ria, "Touch me."

She shook her head.

He guided her hands inside his shirt. Her fingers touched his dark curled hair on his chest. He unbuttoned the rest of the buttons on his shirt and held her fingers on his bare chest. He then quickly helped her remove his shirt.

She kept rubbing her hands on his chest. How she longed for this! All her desires were at its peak. Both her hands started exploring his muscled chest. His fingers went to the hidden zip at the back of her dress. He zipped it down. He was facing her but his hands wandered inside her dress from behind, making her shiver. Her eyes were shut. He saw her moisturizing both her lips with her tongue. He slowly slipped her straps down her shoulders. He freed her breasts from the dress. She wasn't wearing a bra. He looked at her breasts. He wanted to touch them. He watched the nipples grow as one of his fingers touched the tip of it. She gasped. Her breathing increased. He could hear the thumping sound of her heart. He held her waist with both his hands and pulled her closer to him. He kissed her…..hungrily.

A woman like her should be loved and cared for. He had guarded himself from the world but she is the only one who could read him… with a touch. He should have run away from her. But they were connected to each other. He lifted his head and looked at her again. She seemed to be drugged with desire.

Abeer asked, "Ria, do you remember what I told you the last time I kissed you?"

Ria nodded. She remembered everything about him. She blinked her heavy eyelids.

Ria remembered, "You said we'll finish it off when it is all over."

Abeer said, "Right. So, let's finish what was between us. Now it's the time. This is your chance. If you don't want to be touched by me… you may leave my room and go back to yours."

She knew he had no feelings for her. It was just passion between them and nothing more. But then she didn't have a choice. He had always been right about this. There was something between them… an unsaid desire. And she knew… if she leaves now, she would be the biggest fool. He was waiting for her decision but she didn't move. She stood there. Her breasts were bare, waiting to be touched.

She looked into his eyes and said, "I am not going anywhere. I'll stay here."

<h1 style="text-align:center">Chapter 8</h1>

He shut his eyes for a few seconds. He was glad to hear her decision. Her face flushed with desire and he drew her into his arms. She gasped with the reactions of the sparks between them. He knew she had always felt them. He too had, whenever they touched. How he awaited the night they were to meet! They were destined to be here. He moved her dress down from her hips to the floor. He then unpinned her hair. The soft silky hair tumbled over her shoulders. He surveyed her. She looked like a princess from heaven. She was driving him crazy with her looks. He then traced a finger down her one breast and circled the nipple. It hardened. She shivered and gasped. He was satisfied with her reactions. He knew he was doing the perfect justice to her.

Her eyes wanted to remain shut but she forced them open and gazed at him. He had strong desires for her and this made her weak. He controlled his emotions but hers were readable and it gave him that male satisfaction. He was still wearing his pants which guarded him. His mouth went to her neck and he nibbled her with his hot kisses. She moaned and he immediately tongued the bites and soothed the pain. She became aware of the care he was taking for her. She wondered what more feeling could he have, it surely can't be love. Abeer was a hard man with no emotions and she on the other hand was getting emotionally attached to him...to his love.

Her throat was sealed with hot, moist kisses and her head fell back to rest against the wall. Her lips parted slightly and his mouth took control on her. He then started moving down on her breasts and sucked her nipples hard. He sank to his knees, and she felt the hot kisses going down outside of her right thigh and then the inside of it too. He did the same with her left thigh. Her eyes remained closed and her breathing went insane. She could feel his heat through her thin silk panties that she still wore. She cried in joy.

Ria reached for him and he understood her unspoken demand. He stood up and fixed his mouth over hers. They both kissed passionately. The kiss wasn't gentle. It gave more sparks to their cravings. Abeer pressed himself against her, closing all the gaps. He could feel her fingers soothing his bare chest. Her hands went down his biceps and she felt his muscles getting tight with her touch. She evoked the fire inside him. He could sense it. He shuddered and she knew he was losing his control. His mind wasn't obeying his command. Ria had taken control over him. She bent down too and matched his strokes. His hands helped her explore the paths that were more sensitive for pleasure. He closed his eyes. This was more of a fantasy to him. He had fantasized himself many times with Ria. But it was more pleasurable in reality. He suddenly gathered her up in his arms. He walked to the bed and made her lie on it. He then leaned over her without moving his gaze even for a second from her face. She urged to touch him, to stroke his chest but she knew she had to give him the chance now and she obeyed his lips. Her lips parted easily giving him a way to explore her mouth. Her one hand was on his back while the other gave sweet sensations to his chest. The constant electricity between them sent firing currents to his skin giving him arousal sensations.

Abeer pushed himself closer to her. His hands went to her breasts. She knew he wouldn't hurt her physically. But she couldn't control the natural feminine fear of a woman who was lying with a man for the first time. He was much bigger and stronger than her. She shivered with the thought. He bent down his head and took her nipple in his mouth and she gasped at the warm wet suction. Her fingers went to his head and slid through his dark thick hair. She held him closer to her. His mouth went to the nipple of the other breast that he had abandoned a few minutes back. He sucked it. The sweet sensation in her stomach exploded with his suctions. His knee parted her legs apart and he bent down to press her centre. Her hand went desperately over his broad back. She felt his pants on his body. She wanted him to get rid of it but the thought of him being nude over her, made her nervous. With shaky fingers, she touched his zip from the front of his pants and he groaned with pleasure. She got scared and moved her hands off him. He looked at her, and said, "Touch me again." Her mouth went dry but she didn't move.

He took her hand in his and drew the zipper down. She touched the hard male flesh there and he again groaned. This was totally new to her. He gave her the freedom to touch and explore it. He enjoyed her gentle touch. As one of her hands went to the waistband of his pants, he just couldn't control it and immediately took off his pants and threw them on the floor before taking out something from his pant's pocket. He then rolled back to lie on his side to face her.

Ria's eyes went on his masculinity. He shocked her by his heated length. She completely forgot her shyness and her fingers started exploring the veins of his desire. Suddenly she shivered with the thought of him being so huge. Ria's breasts flattened against his chest as he brought her closer to him. He rubbed against hers, enjoying the sensations. He sealed his mouth with hers. Their tongues mated. Their kiss grew more desperate, more demanding as his hands felt her bottom. His fingers moved inside her silk panties and she moaned with pleasure. He pushed her panties off her hips and freed her from all barriers. He broke the kiss. His eyes went down to feast her secrets.

Abeer in a husky voice, "You are beautiful Ria. His hand gently touched her femininity. She shivered. He cupped it with his fingers. He kissed her and she moaned. His fingers went inside to assault her. He parted her femininity and circled it to moisten her with her own desires.

She cried, "Abeeeeerr…." He kissed her more fiercely. Her hands went to his shoulders. He broke his kiss and went down to her breasts and took the nipple in his mouth. His fingers continued to work inside her… and did the magic. She felt a direct sensational connection between her breasts and her thighs. She gave up the idea of fighting with her feelings. She moaned as her muscles tightened. She was getting wild inside. His actions were firm in her. She was reaching for something she had no idea. Abeer whispered, "Don't hold to it. Let it happen. Let go Ria." He kissed her wildly. She cried his name under his lips, "Abeeeerr…." Her body tightened and she landed the pleasure inside her. He released the kiss and smiled at her. He pushed her silky hair on her side. He then gently kissed her all over her face making her feel relaxed. And then she felt him partying her legs as he moved between them. She panicked. She felt drugged. He took her hands in his and guided to his manhood. It was positioned at the opening of her thighs. She wanted him totally. She craved for his body weight on her. She wanted him to be a part of hers. He could feel she was ready now. He didn't wait for any other signal. She greeted him with moist heat in her. As he entered her, he felt her inner muscle stretch to accommodate him. And he entered her completely with one smooth stroke. She couldn't prevent a wild cry. The tearing pain was sharp. But it immediately faded, giving her the other sensations. She could feel him. He was tensed.

He didn't move.

Abeer spoke, "Ria…"

She raised her head and kissed him.

"I am fine now Abeer," she told him.

His mouth again went to hers and he kissed her fiercely. She felt him stretching her with each movement. She was scared but there was no pain. A sweet pleasure was building inside her. His hands went to her breasts and he started fondling them. She gasped with pleasure. He was still moving in her making her go high.

She screamed, "No more Abeer…nooo."

Abeer said, "Let go Ria. Trust me. Take more."

And then he heard her cry. He felt her release but he didn't stop. He didn't let her go and kept moving inside her. He then exploded his climax.

****

Abeer spoke, "You should have told me."

Ria was lying on her side, facing the other way. He had cuddled her with him. He held her very close to him.

Ria said, "You might have stopped."

Abeer said, "No. I wouldn't have. But I would have been more easy on you. I could have hurt you badly."

Ria assured, "You didn't hurt me Abeer."

She knew this was the only thing she would take with her back to her house. This night was hers. He was hers. She had no authority to own him. But the love making that they shared was hers… and it was enough for her for a lifetime. He made her face him and she happily obeyed his new desire. He kissed her passionately. He wasn't convinced by her answer but didn't want to argue with her. He drew her close to him, and they both fell asleep in each other's arms.

****

She woke up first but didn't move an inch away from him. She wanted to enjoy every bit that was left. And then she saw him gazing at her. He kissed her gently on her lips.

Ria spoke, "Abeer….?"

Abeer asked, "Hmm?"

Ria inquired, "Who was Shekhar Oberoi?" Abeer was shocked. He had totally forgotten about her mystical abilities. She bit her tongue for her clumsy words. His body was completely still against hers. Their legs entangled, her breasts pressed against his chest. Apologizing to him, she tried to slip out of his arms. But he tightened his arms around her. He didn't let her slip away.

"Shhh.. where are you going? Stay in my arms," he whispered in her ears. He then kissed her passionately.

Ria apologised, "I am sorry. You need not answer. I just got the thought and you know how it happens and…."

Abeer pacified, "Chill Ria. It's fine." She smiled.

Abeer explained, "He kind of saved me. I was a guy full of temper. I used to be angry at everything….on everyone. I was angry at my mother…for leaving me. I hated my father for what he did. And that guy Saurav… I was angry at him for taking my Aarti away from me. I was angry at my house… for never being my home. I wanted the world to pay for all that I missed. And one day, I took a large stone in my hand and threw it on a man passing by. His head was bleeding but he wasn't angry. He called me and gave me two choices… one – to answer his questions and the second – to call the police and surrender to them. I was only eleven that time. I chose the first. He then asked me all those things that I never wanted to speak about. But I told him everything. He took me to his house. He taught me….. a lot. He was Shekhar Oberoi. A man who taught me how to control my emotions. He taught me how to fight my own battle without harming anyone. And I hope I did justice to him."

Ria knew Shekhar Oberoi was the first man in Abeer's life who taught him how to control. But Abeer lost his childhood behind the walls that he made for himself. She suddenly lifted her head and kissed him on his cheeks. He smiled happily to get distracted from his past. He gave her a warm hug and then both kissed each other breathlessly. Conversations were forgotten. She didn't want to argue and he didn't want to talk. The remaining moments she had left with him were hers. When the time comes for him to leave her, this is what she would have with her. ****

"What the hell? You left her? How could you let Ramya go? Why didn't you call me before freeing her?" Abeer was shocked. He stared at the cops.

The cop said, "She wasn't cooperating with us. We have sent her to another prison and not freed her. There they might take out something from her."

He knew there was nothing he could do now as she had been sent to another country to be questioned and he was not authorized to follow up with her now. He was frustrated. He went back to the hotel and told Ria everything.

Ria asked, "Now what?"

Abeer said, "I have to do something. I'll call the Malaysian police and ask them to send me the information about this woman. I have few contacts there."

She nodded and went to her room. She tried looking for her wallet in her bag. But it wasn't there. She called her granny but the call went unanswered.

Abeer came to her room and asked her why she was so upset. Ria told him about her missing wallet. He told her he'll give her the money that she lost with the wallet and she turned her face from him. She thought Abeer was trying to pay her back for saving Ayaan and she didn't feel happy about it. There was nothing more to the love making they had last night, but surely she didn't want him to do any pay back for her genuine love. She thought she was prepared for what it would be like back home without him. She knew it would be worse than what she thought. She didn't want any uncomfortable scenes when they parted. Abeer owned her nothing.

She was lost in her thoughts when Abeer held her shoulders with his hands. She felt the sparks again by his touch and turned to face him. He whispered sensually in her ears, "Are you tired Ria?" He pushed her hair back over her shoulders and kissed her on her lips and then on her ears.

She shook her head and said, "No. Am not tired." His mouth wandered to her neck. He kissed her throat. She lifted her neck giving him a way to tongue her sensual paths.

Abeer said, "You didn't get much sleep yesterday night."

Ria spoke, "And neither did you."

Her breathing grew unsteady as his hands wandered under her top. And in one go, he took it off. Her breasts were half hidden by her bra. He turned her around and unhooked it, freeing her breasts. He pulled her down to the carpet and fingered her breasts with gentle curls. She was going insane with his touch. She shivered. With shaky fingers, she touched his manhood…. And suddenly they heard the ringing of a phone. He stood up and hurriedly went to his room to pick up the phone.

She calmed her pulse and redressed herself. She went to his room and saw him sitting on the bed with his hands on his forehead. He looked at her and said, "It's time to go back. The agent from Malaysia called up. There is nothing more the woman knows. They are shutting the case. Ayaan is back and that's all that matters now. There is no use hanging around here. She is gone and there is no chance we can talk to her ever again. We only know her name and nothing more than that. I am going back to Mumbai to my family. Once there, I'll make sure Aarti gets divorced from Saurav and gets Ayaan's custody as well."

Ria had no expression on her. Her face was blank. She thought to herself … just a few minutes back, he was being passionate to her and here, now, he says…it's time to go back. She suddenly smiled. Yes… it was time to go back. Abeer looked at her. She seemed unaware of everything around her.

Abeer eyeing her, "Ria…. It's time to go back…" He stood up and came close to her. The colours from her cheeks faded.

Abeer asked, "How about it? Are you ready for a trip back to Mumbai?"

She took a deep breath. It felt as if life had come back to her. There was no reason for her to accompany him. Ayaan was safe. He was with his mother. But he wanted her to accompany him. Of course he didn't love her. He just wanted her to be with him for some more time.

Abeer spoke, "I am sure you are starving. Let's first eat something."

Ria shook her head. He was shocked by her refusal for food. And then she saw him smiling. She knew that expression. It made her bones weak. He walked towards her.

Abeer teased, "You not hungry? Well.. I am. Infact, I am starving."

He caught her and kissed her wildly. She too kissed him back with trembling lips. She was happy…very happy. The colour was back on her cheeks. She had a few more hours with him and these hours were the most precious ones for her. It was more than what she had asked for.

****

Abeer and Ria took a flight to Malaysia instead of going back to Mumbai. Abeer had something else in his mind. They checked into a hotel there.

He called Saket and spoke to him regarding the security. He was happy to hear that Aarti was safe and happy with Ayaan. He also had a heart to heart conversation with his sister. He then handed the phone to Ria as his sister wanted to have a word with her. Aarti thanked her continuously for reuniting her and Ayaan.

Ria felt a little uncomfortable as Aarti made her feel too special. But she was too happy for both Ayaan and Aarti.

They rented a car and announced they were going to the beach. On the way, they went for some swimsuit shopping. It wasn't difficult for them to behave like a normal couple. Looking at them, anyone could assume they were crazily in love with each other. Abeer got a handful of swimsuits for Ria and handed it to her to try on. They were all fancy and seductive. She was reluctant to buy the daring ones. But because Abeer really liked the twopiece modest suit, she took it. It was blue in color. He purchased a black trunk for himself. They drove to the beach. Ria felt happy with the way he cared for her. On the way, Abeer kept checking the rearview mirror, just to be sure no one was following them. At the beach, Abeer found a small deserted place. She was glad that he was careful and made sure she didn't have to be touched by anyone. They sat down on their beach towels that they had purchased.

While sunscreaming her legs, she asked him, "So, whom were you expecting? The other kidnapper? You really think he'll be behind us? Won't he run away somewhere safe knowing that his partner has been prisoned?"

Abeer after a few long minutes, "It's possible. It's difficult to know what he will do next. He might have fled as far as possible. But he might be here as well. There's no way to be sure. But on a second thought… he might be hiding. He may think the police is after him after the woman spilled out all the information about him. There is a possibility. But then there is no way to be sure as we don't know the motive of kidnapping. That's why when we go home, we need to be really careful. He might trace us. We are the only link for him to get Ayaan back."

Ria was listening to every word of his. She applied the sunscreen on her legs. She thought, 'When we go home… that meant when we go home separately…'

Abeer took the lotion bottle from her hands and took a generous amount of it on his palm. He then applied the same on her back. She didn't move. He then moved to her front and applied it on her stomach and the bare area near her breasts. She felt shivers. She enjoyed his touches without expressing anything.

Abeer inquired, "Have you ever been to a beach before?"

Ria replied, "No. My granny never took me anywhere. She is quite possessive about me. And then my abilities too scare her. She knows I'll never be comfortable in a crowd. The mountains have always been my home since my parents left me. I did go down the hill once and my experience was not a happy one."

She frowned. Abeer looked at her quietly. Ria continued, "I was only nine then. A man of about 40, came to meet me at my granny's house. He somehow knew about my visions. He needed help. His son in the army had been missing for over a decade. My grandmother let me go with him.

As soon as he held my hands, I felt discomfort. I wanted to tell my granny…but by then we had left. I went to his house. His wife was there. We were at the dining table when he put his hand on my back… I felt uneasy. Whenever he touched me, I used to get scared. There was something that told me to be away from him… but then I had no one to share my grief with. And the next morning, I saw my granny in the house. She had come back for me. I was very happy to see her. She took me back. I didn't question her. I was glad to be with her and since then I never left the hills. Well.. before I could understand why granny got me back before I even solved the missing issue, I became an adult." Looking at Abeer she continued, "My granny has some mystical powers. She gets to know what's going to take place beforehand. She doesn't need to touch anything for that. It just comes to her."

Abeer could sense her pain. He asked, "Did he hurt you?"

Ria shook her head, "But now I know… he would have, if granny wouldn't have come to my rescue. I owe everything to my granny… everything. She has lived for me."

He took her hands in his and kissed them. He could feel the pain she went through. He didn't let go off her hands. He kept holding them. He suddenly saw her face and immediately left her hands. He understood she again got visions of his past and

he didn't want anyone to know about it. He didn't want to get used to her abilities. But then there was a bond between them and he couldn't deny it. Their physical relationship had made it stronger. Getting physical with her was not love. It was a bodily desire which neither of them could avoid. There was some sort of mystical attraction between them. But knowing she was a virgin, had changed everything. She didn't ask him for anything. No demands from her side. She had given him much more than he desired. This made him uncomfortable. He wanted her to be with him. He was greedy for her company.

It was getting late and so they decided to get back to the hotel. As soon as they reached their floor, they heard the phone ringing in Abeer's room. He went in to pick the call and she went to her room to take a shower. After a hot shower, she got dressed into a top and shorts and went to Abeer's room. He wasn't there. And then she heard the bathroom door open. He came out wrapped in a white towel. His hair was wet. Ria's mouth went dry. He picked a towel from the edge of the bed and started drying his wet hair. Lack of clothes made him more dangerous and the thought made her shiver.

Abeer spoke, "The agent had called. According to him we are not being followed. Good… right?"

Ria nodded, "Hmmm."

He could sense her checking him out. Masculine satisfaction entered him. She was uncomfortable and this thought made him comfortable. Her reactions were readable. He saw her checking him out and turned to face her.

Abeer said, "I don't think you are interested in what I told you about."

Ria spoke, "Of course, I am."

He went close to her. His mouth went closer to hers and gave her a tingling sensation. In a husky voice, Abeer said, "I know you well by now Ria. I know what you are thinking about. I know what you want."

Ria whispered, "Tell me then…."

Abeer brushed his lips against hers and whispered in her ears, "I know.. I know you want… DINNER." She got embarrassed and turned around. He laughed. He teased her.

Ria, getting back to him, "You know Abeer…you are absolutely right. I am soooo hungry. I think I better go down to the restaurant and order something for myself. You can join me if you want but please get dressed first."

Saying this, she turned around and went towards the door to open it. He walked towards her and caught her hand before she got to the door. He pulled her back and drew her against his chest.

Mockingly he said, "You talk about food once more and I'll let go off you."

Ria innocently said, "You just made me realize how hungry I am. It's not my fault."

Abeer whispered, "And what about me.. I am hungry too." He swept her into his arms. "I am very hungry sweetheart. But I had something else in mind…. Something private."

Ria innocently said, "You mean.. a room service…"

Abeer spoke, "Exactly. My room and my service."

He carried her to the bed and dropped her on it. He then climbed the bed and rested over her. He was still smiling at her. This was the first time she saw his playful mood. She thought that from all the memories she'll carry back home, this one would be the most special one. She'll always cherish this. Her expressions told him she was thinking something. He didn't know what. But he knew somewhere he was responsible for her thoughts. His smile faded. He knew she was struggling with her thoughts. His lips touched hers gently and she smiled. She opened her mouth and invited his intimate kiss. The gentleness was all forgotten and their tongues mated. He pulled her top from where it was tucked under her shorts. His hands swept inside it to feel her smooth skin. She shuddered against him as his tongue touched the sensitive part of her mouth. He could feel a deep desire rise in his belly. She responded equally to his desires. This drove him crazy. He wanted everything from her. He wanted to feel her skin burn under his. He wanted her hands to clench on his skin. He wanted her to shiver with desire. He wanted to feel her pulse pounding. He wanted to hear her cry when the passion came to her. He wanted to feel her body getting tight under his. He wanted her to melt in him. He wanted everything. He wanted her today and forever. He wondered…if it would be enough this time.. or would it be enough ever..!!

He crushed his mouth against hers. Her teeth bit his lower lip hinting the desperation in her. He pushed her t-shirt up and cupped her breasts under her lacy bra. His fingers taunted her nipples with his fingers. He left her lips and moved down to her breast. He took a nipple in his mouth and damped her bra. She cried as he took it between his teeth. He suddenly stopped and pulled her t-shirt and bra out of her reach. He then pressed himself on her. He could feel the nipples pricking him as her breasts flattened against his chest. Her hands smoothed his back. The hint of desperation from her gave sparks to his wilder side. He sucked the nipples deeply and batted them with his tongue. She was breathing really fast. Her nails clenched his skin. He zipped down her shorts and opened the buttons on the cloth. He tongued down to taste her navel. He then dragged down her shorts and panties from her long silky legs. He went down to her thighs and pressed his mouth on the most sensual part of hers. She was warm and damp against his mouth. He cupped her bottom as she tried to tighten her legs. She cried. He bent down and nibbled the most sensitive flesh. With lots of care, he entered her with his finger.

She moaned, "Abeeerrr". He lifted her hips towards his mouth. Her hands tangled his hair. Instead of pushing him, she pulled him. He wanted to absorb her. He wanted to feel her. He wanted to touch her. He wanted everything so that he doesn't have the need of wanting her again. He gave her pleasure and she gasped. He heard her repeat his name continuously.

She violently pressed her body against his and he happily sipped her reactions. He entered her with a long smooth shot. She moaned. He didn't let her relax. He didn't want her to relax. He wanted more. He didn't let her melt in his body. He wanted her to get high with pleasure again. He wanted to hear her cries again and again. He wanted to be inside her when his pleasure exploded again. He wanted it to last forever. He wanted to remain inside her forever. His manhood became tight and heavier. Their bodies were stuck to each other. He mouthed her. She screamed as he again went deep into her and they both joined in the pleasure once again and then had the climax together.

They dozed off and woke up again and had another lovemaking session.

The real hunger made them go out for dinner. They returned after midnight and as soon as they reached Abeer's room, he took off his shirt and pulled her down to the carpeted floor. Before indulging himself on her, he pulled her between her legs and brushed her long silky hair. She leaned on him and her hair flowed on his chest. He had always dreamt of this. He then undressed her and they made love even more passionately. They both slept in each other's arms.

****

She was entering the bathroom for a shower. Abeer liked the idea and he was about to follow her when the phone rang. He picked the call and the smile on his face faded.

The agent informed him that Ramya had spilled out all the information. She was not alone. Her partner, Bunny, was at the park too, the day when Ayaan was rescued.

Abeer asked, "Bunny? I have no idea about him."

The agent inquired, "What about your sister? Is it possible?"

Abeer said, "I need to check with her. I am going back to her today itself. Mail me this guy's picture. I shall get back to you on this at the earliest."

The agent said alright and hung the phone.

****

He turned to Ria. She was standing at the bathroom door. She looked pale. Her hands were shivering.

Abeer spoke, "I have to go."

Ria said, "Of course."

Their gazes met. Her face had always been readable to him. But today, it was blank. She looked very pale. With great strength, she asked, "So when are you leaving?"

Abeer answered, "As soon as possible. But we'll have to take lots of precautions as I don't want anyone following us."

Ria, with a smile, "Cool. So I'll pack my bags too. I need to go back to my hills. I just hope I don't get sick on the flight. But whatever it is, I am really excited to get back to my home."

Abeer, without taking his eyes off her, "It seems you are in a hurry to go back.. to your home."

Ria said, "Oh yes. I want to meet granny. The last time I called her she didn't answer the phone. She had plans of visiting her sister. I might even go there to meet her."

Abeer asked, "Won't you like to know what happens to the kidnapper and the real reason behind all this?"

Ria replied, "Of course. I'll wait for your call. I just hope Aarti and Ayaan are completely safe. I think we need to hurry up. I'll go and pack."

She went to her room to pack her bags. He was still. He didn't move. He didn't know what changed but there was something that triggered him. He felt as if someone had drugged him and his brains had stopped working.

****

Granny was still at her sister's house.

Ria felt lonely in her absence. She had called her as soon as she reached her house. She unpacked and cleaned the house and prepared a huge meal for herself but lost the appetite as soon as she sat down to eat.

The plane ride wasn't easy. Abeer had given her 3 sets of tickets out of which two were just plotted so that if she is being followed, her actual destined flight gets her safely to her town. He made all the arrangements for her so that she has no problems. He also gave her some money to which she frowned. But he convinced her to take it as it was not for her credits but only for the expenses that she would incur on her way back to the hills. It was time for the departure.

Ria's flights were announced. Abeer came closer to her. She skipped a heartbeat thinking he might kiss her. But he didn't. She was afraid to be touched by him. She might get weak and if she does get weak, he'll know what she has been hiding. No. She won't let him pity her. Taking a deep breath, she smiled and bid him goodbye. Turning gracefully, she walked away. She didn't even turn once to check if he was still standing. She wanted to see him again. How she wished, she could see him one last time. But she knew he wouldn't be there and she didn't want to hurt herself. She boarded the plane last. She became uncomfortable seeing the passenger sitting beside her. But at least this made her forget Abeer for a while.

****

She washed the dishes and recleaned the house. She felt lonely. At once she went to her room and repacked her bags. She planned to go to her granny and stay there. She didn't want to be alone. She was sure her granny wouldn't ask any questions. And this would give her some time to figure out a way to live the rest of her life without Abeer Singh.

****

Abeer sat on the couch with Aarti. Ayaan was sleepy. He was happy to see Abeer and didn't want to go for his afternoon nap. But then his nanny forced him to sleep.

Abeer then spoke to the agent and checked his mails for the second kidnapper Bunny's picture. He took out the print of the same. Holding Aarti's hands in his, he told her all about the search and how Ayaan was rescued. She was still. He then told her about the kidnapper Ramya who had now given them her partner's lead.

Aarti inquired, "What's his name?"

Abeer replied, "Bunny is the name and here is his picture. Do you know…."

Aarti said shockingly, "Bunn ..Bunny… ohh God.." She started sweating. Her face went white.

Shaking her, Abeer asked, "Do you know him? How? Who the hell is he? Tell me Aarti.."

Her lips were trembling. "What will happen now Abeer? What will we do? He will find us…I always knew this.."

He ordered, "Aarti, tell me who is this BUNNY?"

Looking at him with teary eyes, she said, "He works for Saurav. He was also there the night you rescued me."

Abeer calmed her. Aarti continued, crying, "Now we'll never never never be safe. He'll get us. Saurav will get us."

Abeer pacified her, "Calm down Aarti. I swear to you, I won't let anything happen to you and Aayan. You both will be safe. Now wipe those tears off your face and listen to me carefully."

Aarti calmed herself. She wiped her tears and had some water. Taking a few deep breaths, she nodded to Abeer to continue. Abeer taking one of her hands in his, he said, "Ramya and Bunny have been together for the past one year. They have been in a relationship. Ramya knows nothing about his past. When she met him, he was a baggage handler at one of the counters in Mumbai Airport. A week before Ayaan was kidnapped, he didn't return home. And when he did, he had plans. He told Ramya they will be rich soon."

Aarti said, "Oh no.. that means he saw me…at the airport…the day I came to surprise you with Ayaan at the arrival gate."

Abeer said, "I think that's how he traced you. You have cost him his job."

Aarti nodded, "Yes. I am sure. Saurav won't have spared him. He would have…" She shivered.

Abeer said, "But he is still roaming free. This means he must have fled as soon as he found out you were missing. He didn't wait to face Saurav."

Aarti said, "But when he recognized me, he could have taken me back to him. He didn't have to take Ayaan. Bunny knows how much hatred Saurav has for kids. He could have gone back to Saurav to be in his good books again. Saurav would have been generous enough to him for letting him know my whereabouts.
This doesn't make much sense, Abeer".

Abeer said, "Saurav hates kids. But not your in-laws Aarti."
She stared at her brother. Aarti said, "You mean….he…"

Abeer spoke, "Ramya said Bunny was delighted to find out about Ayaan. He at once called your in-laws and told them all about your little secret. He knew how desperately Saurav's parents wanted their grandchild. He at once demanded a huge amount to pass Ayaan to them. And they happily agreed."

Aarti said, "Bunny is still free. We are not safe Abeer. He'll try his hands again on Ayaan. We'll have to hide for the rest of our lives."

Abeer shook his head, "No Aarti. No one will believe him. Saurav wont spare him as he let you escape and ran off to save his life from him. And now, your in-laws too won't believe him as he doesn't have Ayaan with him. He is at a loss. And please…trust me. Stop worrying. I'll make sure we never have to worry about Bunny or your bastard husband ever again. I'll finish this off forever."

Abeer didn't have any plans. He didn't know how he'll be accomplishing it. But he knew he would find a solution. He won't fail now. The lives of his sister and nephew were in his hands.

Chapter 9

Spending a few days with her granny had surely made her forget her loneliness. She felt good. But returning back to her house alone, made her relive the thoughts that she wanted to dump somewhere in the corner of her heart. She didn't want to return back without her granny. But there was this lady who needed her help in finding some court documents that she had misplaced and had to file them immediately. So she made her trip back to the hills.

She went to the pharmacy and refilled the pain medication which was needed now. Back at her house, she busied herself. She cleaned, wiped the wooden floors, did the laundry, ironed the damp clothes and also cleaned the garden area. She did everything she could lay her eyes on. She had prepared herself well for their parting.. but she was wrong. There was a huge vacuum in her. She had no feelings for herself too. She became a machine. There was too much pain in her. The pain of being alone was too intense. It was slowly killing her. But she knew she was doing the right thing. Abeer was not in love with her. He wanted her company and nothing more than that. He had built a huge wall around himself throughout his life. She knew he'll never be comfortable with a woman like her.. a physic who could read him even with a small touch. She didn't blame him. But the pain was too large and was now getting uncontrollable.

She cooked herself a gigantic dinner and was happy to finish it off. Maybe meeting her granny for a while did smoothen her discomfort. She was washing the dirty dishes when she heard a knock on her front gate. She peeped out of the window and saw a stranger standing with a car in her driveway. She opened the door slightly leaving the chain on, just to be careful as it was pretty dark outside. Her house being in an isolated area, she knew she always had to be careful.

The man spoke, "Hello miss.. ahh well.. I was passing by.. and my car is having some trouble…"

He smiled at her and continued, "Please it would be really kind if you could guide me to some mechanic nearby. It's late and pretty cold too." She looked at the man carefully. He seemed harmless to her.

Ria said, "I am sorry. But the nearest mechanic's hut shuts by afternoon. You won't get him until tomorrow morning."

The man inquired, "And how far is a lodge from here? I can't keep sitting in the open to freeze myself."

Ria answered, "Well… it's about two kilometers from the left."

He checked his watch and then shook his head. He started walking back to his car and tried starting it. But it wasn't responding. And then after a few more attempts, she saw him heading back in his car. Surely the car was making a weird sound. She just hoped he reached the lodge safely.

Ria shut the door properly and went back to the kitchen to clean the mess that she had left in between. She washed the utensils and dried them with a towel. But her mind kept going back to the little conversation she had with the stranger. She kept all the utensils back in their designated place. She cleared the planks and stacked the cutleries back. She then picked the knife and…the memories hit her… the watch.. it was golden in color.. …and she became still and then she started shivering.

She remembered - 'A toddler she could see… he was sitting on a huge bed and was getting fascinated by a blue light… he was smiling at the light and wanted to hold it… whenever the kid tried to hold the light, a huge hand would grasp him and push him back to the middle of the bed…'

Yes, it was this hand. She had not seen the kidnapper's face. But his hand… she could not forget. He wore a gold watch around his wrist. But then there could be more hands with similar watches. She felt foolish. How could she link two different situations to one… this can be a mere coincidence. She peeped through the window to check if the stranger with his car could be seen. But he wasn't visible. The sky was painted black. After several foolish minutes, she turned back and went to where the phone was kept. She picked the receiver and dialed Abeer's number and then dropped back the receiver in its place. How could she become so weak? She forced herself back to the kitchen and started cleaning the cupboards which didn't need any assistance. She had made sure of holding her tears back when they had parted. She didn't want to beg him to be hers forever. Calling him now would make her a coward in her eyes. She wanted to hear his voice desperately but not at the cost of her pride. She didn't want to force herself on him. She knew very well, had she wanted, she could have made him feel something. She knew that masculine possessiveness he had, every time he looked at her in the last few days. He cared for her. But then he was possessive about his sister and nephew too. He cared about them too. But she wanted much more than that. And she knew he'd never give her what she wanted.

She had accepted the truth. But this truth hurt her. It was her life's irony. She kept away from all the people around her for a long time, as she didn't want anything physical or intimate with any of them. But with Abeer, it was different. From the very beginning, on the hills, she was aware of it and never even denied it. She was always scared of it as she knew her powers would destroy her if she got physical. But Abeer made her know herself.

With him there was no fear.

Her spine ached. She was tired cleaning the house. Unconsciously, she again went to the window and peeped through it. There was nothing unusual. She moved away from it.

She stared at the telephone. She wanted to speak to her granny. The thought made her feel comfortable and she picked the receiver to dial. There was no response from the other side. She cut the dial and waited for the dial tone to come so that she could redial the number. But the realization hit her.

The phone was dead. Her fingers became numb. She was scared. She dreaded the silence in her house. It wasn't the first time that she was home alone. But today, she was afraid. She didn't know why… but there was something which wasn't right. She kept the receiver back and ran to the main door to check if it was locked properly. The chain was on. She put the double lock for safety. Then she checked each window in her house. They were all locked and nicely covered with the blinds. There were no more doors in the house. The basement had a door to outside but that was covered with thick double doors as they never opened it. All the vegetables that granny canned over the year were all stored there. She came back to the kitchen, checked if everything was in place. The living room too seemed to be still. The silence grew deeper and she started shivering. She reassured herself that everything was fine. The phones were dead sometimes. But her logical reasonable mind warned her.. and she felt goosebumps.

And then she heard some noise outside. She froze. But the sound wasn't repeated. Her house, being located at a deserted part of the town, no sound of any vehicle or animals could be heard. She swallowed her breath. She heard another sound again. This time she ran to her bedroom window and peeped out. She saw nothing. She turned off all the lights in her house and went back to her bedroom and sank on her bed. She was getting all weird thoughts. The stranger knocking her door… the kidnapper's hand… the gold watch… the dead phone… the noise outside her house…

She was shivering. She didn't know the reason. She kept looking at the main door from time to time. She got out of her room and took the keys of her car in her grip. She wanted to unlock the main door and run to her car, turn it on and speed away from her house to a more secured area. She moved towards the door and stopped. She thought to herself… what was she exactly running from? Who was she running from? She had no answer.

And then she heard the noises again. Her peace was shattered. She listened intently for the sound thinking it could be her imagination. But they were real. Someone was outside. She could hear the sound of someone tapping the door of the basement. Her heart sank.

****

Abeer and Saket were sitting on the coffee table engrossed in the conversation.

Saket asked, "So we don't know where Bunny is?"

Abeer shook his head, "No. He could be anywhere. He could have hid himself. But you never know…he could be in this city too."

Saket said, "He is too smart, Abeer. Don't forget he had drugged Aarti and fled away with Ayaan. No one even saw him doing that. He didn't leave a trace. He is very clever."

Abeer said, "I think he was just lucky. When Aarti collapsed, a huge crowd gathered around her and Bunny along with Ramya took the advantage. He did the same at the park. He knew he would be caught when I gripped Ramya's forearm. He didn't waste a second and vanished. Although the police have been after him, he is still roaming free."

Saket said, "The police couldn't even trace the kidnapping of Ayaan. They had almost shut the case. But Ria took it forward. She didn't let the kidnappers fool her."

Abeer spoke, "Hmmm… they couldn't fool Ria." He didn't want to think about her. He didn't want Saket to remind him of

Ria. He had already lost too much sleep thinking about her. Everytime he lay on his bed, he felt tortured. The memory of her being naked under the silk black sheets…. He wasn't sure if it was his memory or a so-called vision… but he felt the pain… and he shifted restlessly in his chair.

Saket asked, "When did you last speak to Ria?"

Abeer didn't answer. He had always used his charm on women he wanted. It was too easy for him to get those women under him. But his charm didn't help him with Ria. She gave him more than he asked for, and in return, she wanted nothing from him. She easily bid him goodbye too. The thought made him angry. It was so damn easy for her to walk out from him. Their relation was just a casual affair for her. She acted as if they never had anything between them. Of course he was in a hurry to get back to where his sister was, he wanted to reach her at the earliest so that he could tell her all about Bunny. But that didn't mean he planned to go alone. He wanted Ria to come with him. But she turned away from him without even knowing what he really wanted. She had squashed him. It was too easy to mention her home to him. She wanted to get back to the hills and didn't even think about him once. She didn't even think about what they had between them. All she wanted was to finish the mission and leave and she was in such a hurry that going by flight too didn't bother her much. She didn't even turn once to check if he was still waiting for her. He wanted her to accompany him. He didn't want her to leave him. She always understood him but why not this time. He hated her. The anger made him grow mad. He didn't want to think about her. She betrayed him. He had never chased any woman in his life and he will never chase her too. But the feeling that he was left with, at the airport, was unusual. He felt that something precious that was his, was being snatched from his grasp.

How the hell did she manage to be so cool? Not one backward glance? She didn't think about him once? She didn't even hug him before leaving. A goodbye wave and a smile – was it enough? Just the memory made him clench his jaws. He knew it wasn't just the sex they had. It was much more than that. She was a virgin. She couldn't pretend that their time together hadn't meant something to her. He was the first man she trusted and willingly gave herself to him. She trusted him enough to make love to her. Then why? Why did she go? Was she afraid? Was she afraid of being so well connected with him? He too was afraid of the bond they shared. But now she had enough time alone to think over it. He won't grant her more time. She had to face him now.

Saket (interrupting his thoughts), "Abeer? Did you speak to her even once after returning back?"

Abeer replied, "No….."

Saket asked, "No what? You didn't speak to her? She helped us get Ayaan back. What the hell is wrong with you?"

Abeer leaned his head on the chair and stared at the ceiling. Saket pulled his chair next to him and shook him. He knew his friend was up to something… something that was dangerous.

Saket inquired, "I am asking you again Abeer. Did you speak to Ria?"

Abeer replied, "No. Actually I had called her twice today. But she didn't pick my calls."

Saket looked at him. He still wasn't sure that Abeer made the effort of speaking to her.

Abeer further explained, "I did call her once in the morning but she didn't answer and then before coming here, I had again dialed her. But her phone was no longer in service."

Saket said, "That's a little odd. Isn't it?"

Abeer gave a thought to it. He wasn't sure if it was odd but he definitely hated the idea of not being able to hear her. He wanted to talk to her once. He knew they had something mystical between them and he won't let her forget it. No matter what happens, he'll make sure he gets her back.

Abeer spoke, "Actually she lives in a deserted area with her grandmother. Maybe her phone lines went bad."

Saket said, "You mean she is not in the main town? Is the area too isolated?"

Abeer spoke, "Yes, very. Though she lives with her grandmother, but Ria had mentioned that her granny won't be around for a few weeks. She is on a visit to her sister's place."

But something made him uneasy. The thought of Ria being alone in the deserted area, in her house, made him feel uncomfortable.

Saket said, "Hmmm. Maybe she too went to visit them and that's why the phones are being unanswered. But don't you think she would want to know what happened when you got back here? She didn't even call once to enquire whether Aarti is associated with the kidnappers. Don't you think it's a little unlike her? Won't she like to know what happens to Bunny or whether Ayaan is still safe? I think she would be interested in knowing Bunny was a former employee of Saurav. She is probably going crazy wondering what's going on and here we are just...."

Abeer interrupted, "Oh God..!!!"

Saket gave Abeer a strange look and said, "Look Abeer. I think you should contact her. I know there is something between the two of you and you will be the biggest fool if you just let her go."

But Abeer wasn't listening to Saket. His thoughts were somewhere else. He was getting scared. He frowned at his thoughts. A thought was forming in his mind. A horrible one. He suddenly stood up and picked the phone from a nearby table. He dialed Ria's number and the recording informed him that the lines were out of service. He banged the phone back on its place. He was angry at himself. He was frustrated and scared.

Saket stood up from his chair and went to him. He pacified him, "Calm down Abeer. The phone lines will get fixed soon. Stay cool."

Abeer turned around to face his friend and said, "Saket, I don't think I mentioned this to you. But Ria's wallet from her bag had been missing since the day we rescued Ayaan."

Saket said, "Big deal Abeer. I am sure you must have replaced the money that she lost. So why are you thinking about it now?"

Abeer took a deep breath in. He shook his head and looked at Saket. Abeer said, "Ramya had mentioned to the police that Bunny was with her at the park. But when Ria created havoc there, he fled away. But…but what if he didn't ….?"

Saket asked, looking puzzled, "What if he didn't what?"

Abeer impatiently said, "What if he didn't leave the park?"

He remembered how he had found Ria in the middle of the huge crowd. He remembered how she was holding the stroller with the most precious gift inside. He then had his focus only on Ria and Ayaan. But now all the pieces were settling in their place.

Abeer continued, "He was there. He might have faded in the crowd. But I am sure he didn't go far. He stayed back and watched the whole scene. Of course we didn't know he was there and so he didn't have to worry about anything unless Ramya spotted him. But he very well knew she won't point him. He saw everything. He saw us going with the security guards. I had forgotten about her bag. When we left, it was still at the rescue point."

Saket was shocked, "And her wallet was in her bag."

Abeer nodded. He was angry at himself for being so stupid. Saket looked worried. Abeer said, "Her diving license…her address. I didn't think of it once also. Goddddd…"

Without wasting a second, he marched to his room. Aarti, who was coming to check on them, was tensed to see his speed and the frustrated look on his face. Both Saket and Aarti followed him to his room. He started packing his suitcase while giving orders to Saket, "Call the securities now. Tell the Head to get to Ria's place now. Ask them to get her out of her house to a secured place right away. Use your contacts. And yes, book the private jet. I need to fly as soon as I reach the airport. Also make arrangements for a vehicle once I reach there. I'll be needing one to rush to her place. I hope you have got everything under you Saket. Don't mess it up."

Saket nodded. Aarti was shocked. She kept looking at both the men. She knew that look on Abeer's face. She had seen the same terrible look when Ayaan was kidnapped.

Aarti asked, "Abeer, tell me what happened? What's wrong? Is it Ria? Is she fine? Where is she? What's happening? Is she in some trouble?"

Abeer turned to face her and said in a loud voice, "I hope not. I won't let anything happen to her." And he walked out of the house....

Chapter 10

Ria was shivering. Hours passed and the noise kept going on. She knew the threat in her consciousness was about to materialize. Her mind was numb. She was sure about the stranger now. She knew it's him who is trying to break through the basement door. It's him who had kidnapped Ayaan. He had traced her. She didn't know how, but he was there. She was alone in an isolated house. There was no way she could seek help. The only person she could now rely on was she… herself.

She had nothing to protect her. She calmed her fears. She had no options. There was no point running out of the front door to the car. She knew if she did so, he would easily get hold of her. This means she'll have to stay there and wait for him. She took a deep breath and waited. Every passing minute was making her nervous. But she had to keep a good hold on herself. She didn't want to break down.

He was getting closer to her. Any moment he could be there. She faded her thoughts. It wasn't the time to worry about how or what he'll do with her. It was time to think about how she will keep herself alive. She very well knew the kidnapper had come to her to know where Ayaan was. She was the only one who could give him the information. And once she told him about Ayaans whereabouts… he'll surely get rid of her.

She started searching for weapons that would help her. But there was nothing more than the kitchen knives. She got hold of them but she knew she won't be able to use them. If she tried those on him, she would land up touching him. He would surely try taking the knives off her hands. And if she touches him, all his evil thoughts and emotions will get transferred to her.

Finally her eyes went to the cane sticks that granny had secured over the last few years as her collection. One of them had a brass handle. She quickly picked it up and went to the switchboard. She turned off the last lamp in the house. She then moved to the staircase from where the kidnapper shall be coming once he broke through the basement door. She stood behind one of the walls there and waited for him. She knew he would see her as soon as he came up. But she had no choice. She had to stand there in order to hit him first before he made any attempts. She knew he would also be having a weapon with him. But she had to take the chance.

The basement door fell apart. She could hear the creak sound. She knew he had come in. She couldn't allow herself to be fearful now. This was the final moment when she'll need all her strength to save herself.

For one last time she blinked and smiled to herself. How she wished she could see him once! Abeer… the man who took so long to trust her and her abilities. She won't let his trust break. She won't let him fail. She won't risk the little boy Ayaan's life again. She focused on Abeer. His love gave her strength. She could hear the man climbing the stairs one by one. It didn't take him much time to get to the last stair. The wait was over. The kitchen door opened. She hit him hard with the stick. He was carrying a gun which flew from his grip with a tearing sound and landed on the kitchen floor. The man hit the ground.

She was shivering. She still had the stick firmly in her hands. She stood there. She wanted to run but had no energy. The man didn't move. She wondered.. had she killed him? She knew it was the best opportunity for her to run away. But she bent down a little to check whether he was alive. She could hear him breathing. She then took back her place. Slowly she started to move back. She had to get to the front door to free herself from him. And then.. she felt his fingers around her ankle. She screamed. She got the evil thoughts from his fingers. He was an evil man who had killed many before. It didn't matter to him if the person was of his use or not. He killed anyone who came in this way. And she was now his present target.

She hated the thoughts that travelled to her from the touch of his fingers. He tried to stand up. The gun shot had touched his forearm and he recollected his strength to teach her a lesson. He will kill her for sure. But he wanted to go slow on her now. He wanted to give her pain. He wanted to show her how cruel he is. He won't spare her. He'll show the real world to her. He won't leave her even if she pleads with him to. She yelled again. He held her tightly and tried coming up to level her. She started panting. She took the stick up and brought it down again with all her strength and hit him hard on his head. She repeated the act unconsciously several times. She could feel his hold getting weak on her. She struggled to let go but he didn't leave the grip. She had to get away from him. His evil side was getting to her nerves. Her head started spinning. She started getting pain in her temples. She didn't want to fail herself. She brought the stick once more to his wrist and hit him hard. He left the grip. She freed herself from his grip and more than that, from the evil visions that got into her head.

She took a deep breath in. The freedom from the visions made her relive again. Her numb body started breathing again. But she felt dizzy. She ran towards the front door banging into the furniture which was static throughout. With shaky fingers she tried opening the locks and the chain of the door. She was scared with the thought of having the evil hands back on her. She had to get away at the earliest. She struggled and finally the lock opened. She ran out of the door and made her way through the bushes. Her hands were bleeding as she cut through the bushes and the trees. Her clothes were torn but she didn't care. She just had to run as fast as she could so that she reached a secured place. She wanted to be away from that man and suddenly she had more energy than ever to get help for herself. Without caring about her bleeding hands, legs, neck and back, she kept running. She cried and cried for help.

****

The cops were there. Her house was surrounded by uniformed men. The lights of the police van killed the colours of the night. Abeer came out of his rented car and ran towards her house. One of the policemen got hold of him and asked, "Who are you?"

Abeer demanded, "Where is Ria?"

The policeman spoke, "Huh.. I am the one who'll be asking questions. Now answer me… Who are you? And what do you want?"

Abeer said, "Look.. I am the one who called your office and got you here. Now tell me…where the hell is Ria? Is she here? Is she fine?"

But he didn't get any answers. Angry at himself, he started walking towards the door of the house. Now he himself would check. He kept repeating, 'Nothing can happen to her. She will be safe. She must be in her room. She must be sleeping. I am thinking too much.'

The cops got pissed and two of them started following him. One of them said, "Hey you.. come back. You cannot get in there."

Abeer kept walking at full speed. He didn't care about anyone. He just wanted her to be safe. His eyes were searching for her. He looked everywhere and as he was about to step in, his eyes saw something. He ran towards it. He reached the place and stopped at a distance from where she was sitting. He felt his heartbeat. Yes…she was very much alive.

Abeer spoke, "Ria Mehta…"

She was talking to a cop. She turned around and couldn't believe her eyes. She saw Abeer. He was walking towards her like a dream. She didn't move. She kept gazing at him. She was scared to utter a word from her mouth or to move towards him. She thought if she takes one step ahead, he might get dissolved. And then she felt his strong arms around her. He hugged her tightly. He bent down and kissed her on her lips. She felt the connection. He kissed her hard and she too responded to his kiss. The shawl that covered her shoulders slid down as she placed her arms around Abeer's neck. She didn't even care about the cloth. He hugged her tightly. But she knew the hug wasn't tight enough... she could never get close to him.

Ria said, "Abeer...." She looked at him. He was for real. She couldn't believe it. But she was glad. ********
The policeman came up to them. He angrily asked Ria, "Are you alright?" She nodded. He turned to face Abeer and raised his voice, "Look mister.. You are not supposed to enter the crime scene. This is not a park that you guys can just barge in and...."

Abeer didn't care about the cop. All he cared about was Ria and her safety. He was now convinced she was safe. He moved back to look at her from head to toe. His jaws tightened as his gaze moved down her body. Her clothes were torn. She had bruises all over her skin. Her soft silky hair that he loved was all tangled. She was in a mess. He could feel the pain she went through. He froze.

Ria whispered, "He came here to get me..." Tears started running down from her eyes, down to her cheeks. Taking a deep breath, she continued, "I couldn't get away. I couldn't call anyone for help. I was alone in the house. I had to fight him off and then he touched me and I saw...." She started shivering. With shaky lips she said, "Abeer.. Abeer.. I had to hit him. I hit him again and again... and I just couldn't get away..."

He drew her towards him. Her face leaned against his chest. He could feel her breathing very fast. He held her tight and smoothened her back with his hands.

She whispered, "I thought I had killed him."

Abeer spoke, "I really wished you had."

His voice made her comfortable. She felt heaven in his arms. She felt secure with him. The horrible experience of the late evening, slowly drifted and she started to breathe normally.

The police lined up questions that needed to be answered by both of them. They took turns and answered the cops. Ria was exhausted and seeing her pale face, Abeer put an end to them.

Abeer said, "Ria needs rest. I need to take her to the doctor as well. We have given you enough stories to get that guy behind the bars. If you need me again, do give me a call and I'll be there."

The policeman looked at them. He then told Ria, "You may rest now. We are leaving but shall return in the morning. Though both of you have given us more information than what we require, I'll still have to come up to check the evidence in the house left behind by that fellow. Though he has gone, we'll need all that's in there to lay our hands on him. Till then, take care."

The cops also told them not to fiddle with any evidence at the crime scene. They nodded. Abeer didn't want to offend the cops. He was glad that the cops were here before the bastard could lay his evil hands on Ria. He knew it was Saket who called them and made them rush to save Ria. One of the officers had rescued her when he saw her stumbling on the road. He requested them to go there in full speed to protect her. How he wished he was there to protect her! He hated himself for making her suffer. The fact that he wasn't there with her when she needed him the most, would haunt him for the rest of his life.

As soon as the police went off, Abeer took Ria's hands in his and started to walk up the stairs to her house. He sensed her discomfort while getting into her house. They entered through the front door. All the lights in the house were on. The living room was still. There was no movement of any furniture in there. He could see some blood on the floor in the kitchen area. By the look of Ria in the torn outfit and the bruises on her skin, he was prepared for what awaited in the kitchen area. But then his gaze fell on the little hole on one of the walls and he froze.

She looked at the direction of his gaze. Ria explained, "He had a gun. It flew off his hands when I hit him for the first time. He couldn't spot it in the dark. The cop found it under the dining table." And then her face started getting pale. There were no expressions on it. She started to shiver. The thought of what happened there, just a couple of hours back, made her shiver. She realized what could have happened to her. He saw her face. He knew the trauma she went through. He could sense all her cries and helplessness. But now… she was safe and she was with him. ********

Abeer still couldn't absorb the fact that she stood right in front of him, in one piece. He tightened his arms around her as he fought for control. She welcomed his hug. She had craved it. She knew only his touch could make her forget the hours of struggle with the evil man. She wanted to lose herself in him. She wanted this and more. She wanted to be convinced that the nightmare was over. She lifted her head to kiss him. He crushed her lips with his. The desire once again started flowing. His thoughts and strong desires passed through his touch to her senses. She froze with the awareness of the emotions that he had for her.

Coming back to her senses, she started unbuttoning his shirt. Her shaky fingers couldn't finish the task and Abeer helped her complete it. The current between their skins started making them weak. With clumsy fingers, he unbuttoned her top and freed her bra. He bent down to her breasts and sucked both the nipples till they became hard. She could feel his wet hot mouth teething her nipples and she cried with desire. She moaned. She gasped. He then caught her flurry skirt and raised it above her thighs. The night was cold and Ria shivered as the cool breeze in her house rushed over her thighs and breasts. She gasped. Somehow she managed to remove his opened shirt and her hands clenched his bare chest. He started moving her backward, his chest hair brushing her breasts. His mouth was stuck to hers as she moved backwards and she felt the table at the back of her hips.

Abeer's hands went under her skirt and he pulled down her panties. She shivered as his hands moved between her legs. He lifted her and made her sit at the edge of the table and moved between her open thighs. Both their hands made their way to the button and the zipper of his pants. He allowed her to free his manhood and her fingers started to explore the length of it.

Abeer in a hoarse voice, "Now. Ria I want to be inside you now." The passion flowed. She guided his length to the warm damp sensual part of hers. He entered it with one desperate shot. She moaned. She gasped. She cried with passion. She opened her drowsy eyes and gazed at him. He was still inside her. His eyes were shut. His hands went to her hips and he re-entered her with a heavy thrust. This time he went deep inside her. There were only sensations. Her breasts flattened against his chest as he covered her mouth with his. Their tongues mated while he pressed her breasts. Her hands gripped his shoulders. His mouth was hard and demanding. She readily gave the desire to him. He kept reentering her with heavy desire. Their hips battled with each other.

She kept moaning as his breathing went harsh. He could feel her body tighten and he increased his rhythm, getting into her everytime with extra force. He felt her legs behind his back.

She cried, "Abeeerrr…" and he shuddered inside her forcefully. He threw inside her as she too had her climax and the passion made her relive again. They were inseparable. They were divine.

Their muscles started to relax after the brutal passion. Abeer slipped out of her carefully and gathered her in his arms. He then took her to her bedroom and made her lie down on the bed. He then undressed her completely. She kept looking at him without even blinking once. He stood up and took off his pants. It was amazing how the desire in both of them made them ONE, without even getting off the clothes completely.

Another minute passed and he was under the quilt with her. He slowly pressed his body weight on her as she hugged him tightly. He pulled her closer to him and caressed her spine. He then touched her tangled yet soft hair and kissed them. He knew the soft silky hair of hers, now belonged to him.

She whispered, "Why did you come here?"

He didn't answer and she didn't even bother. All she knew was, he was there with her. He was there when she needed him. He was holding her close to him. She could hear his heartbeats. She felt safe and secured in his arms.

Ria spoke, "Abeer… I need to tell you something. That man…"

Abeer whispered back, "Shhh..hh..hh… Just sleep sweetheart. Just sleep."

He held her in his arms until she slept. He could hear her deep relaxed breaths. He didn't leave her even after she dozed off. He just wanted her to be close to him, to be in his arms. The realization of how easily he could have lost her tonight, kept coming back to him. He couldn't part with her. He didn't mind being awake for the rest of the hours, holding her close to him, while she slept.

He just knew one thing… that no matter what… He won't let go off her again. Never ever again.

Chapter 11

Ria and Abeer both relished their breakfast. Ria had prepared pancakes for both of them. Abeer was not bothered about the number of pancakes she consumed. Although he had less than half of what she grabbed, he was almost double of her weight. He knew she needed a good heavy meal to pull off her visions. He thought to himself, what if she gains weight, how will he lift her? And he smiled…

Ria was still digging into her pancakes when her gaze fell on his lips. The corner of his mouth had little crumbs settled on them and she slowly got up from her seat and licked them. Her eyes met his. A warm satisfaction lingered in her, as his eyes followed every movement of hers.

In a husky voice, Abeer spoke, "If you are trying to seduce me, then let me tell you, I am all ready to get back to the bed with you. But I don't think it's a good idea to have the cops barging in the house while we get cozy unless you want them to check on us.

So what's your call?"

Ria frowned, as last night's evil memory hit her again.

Ria said, "I think I have done something illegal."

Abeer looked at her with a mocking smile. He was calm and made a lovable gesture. The look on his face made her realize how badly she had missed him. She had never thought they would ever make love again and suddenly there was a wave of emotions inside her.

Abeer said, looking into her eyes, "I don't think I can ever see you in the raw ladies gang. You are not their type. You are more to be possessed. Well.. so what exactly did you do to go against the law?"

Ria, taking a deep breath in, said, "Well… that man… who broke in… was… he was the other…."

"Kidnapper…" Abeer completed. "I know that Ria. And I am really sorry. It took me a while to put the pieces together. His name is Bunny.. Bunny D'souza."

Ria whispered, "He worked for Saurav."

Abeer said, "He worked. Not anymore. He was his bodyguard. But he failed when Aarti escaped. He must have fled away."

Ria said, "But he won't rest until he gets Ayaan back."

Abeer said, "So that's why he came up here. He wanted Ayaan's new location. He must have grabbed your wallet at the park. That's how he must have traced you up here."

He thought- 'How dumb he was to think that someone was following them all the while in Malaysia while this man had already planned how to reach Ria when she comes back to her house.' He was as angry at the kidnapper as he was at himself. Seeing the anger on his face, Ria covered his hands with hers and said, "Please don't blame yourself."

Abeer said, "How could I have been such an idiot? I should have figured out this much earlier. I was so excited to have found Ayaan that I completely neglected the missing wallet that had all your IDs in it." She knew his nature was not to forgive himself. He blamed everything on him and that's how he had become a hard man earlier. But not anymore. She won't let him take all the blame on him. Ria sternly said, "Stop it Abeer. You are not God, that you need to be perfect in everything. All of us have flaws. Stop living in guilt for every damn thing. You are not born to please everyone. Live for yourself sometime. Make mistakes. It's healthy to make mistakes. Stop carrying the burden of guilt. We are all responsible for ourselves. Accept this and go on. Let go of your sorrows."

Abeer raised his eyebrows and asked her, "Hey, have you been talking to Aarti?"

Ria answered, "No. Why?"

He shook his head. He said, "Well… the two of you have a lot in common."

Ria said, "Hmm… Abeer, that guy Bunny was just not a bodyguard. He was a hired killer. I think it was he who worked for Saurav and killed all those his master ordered. He is dangerous. He has killed many innocent people. We need to find him. We need to get him behind the bars. It's important for us. We need to do this...for Aarti… for Ayaan." Abeer was quiet. He was listening to every word she spoke. And then she said, "I know how to find him."

Abeer inquired, "And how? Tell me Ria. Tell me exactly what is going on in your mind."

Ria spoke, "Yesterday… when Bunny came into my house…I didn't escape him at one shot. He had grabbed me… my ankle. He was drowsy due to the pain the stick in my hands gave him. But I still got a scene from his past. This scene matched the one I sensed when Saurav had touched me in the musical academy at Singapore." Abeer's face froze. He kept looking at Ria. And then after a handful of seconds, he asked her to tell her everything she knew.

Ria said, "Okay.. so they were four of them… Saurav, Bunny, another guy and the victim Hasan. They were in a construction area. And then I saw Hasan lying on the ground in a pool of blood."

Abeer asked, "You know the victim's name as well..." He surveyed her and said, "This means he is loaded with criminal acts. He is just not a kidnapper but a murderer too. And if Bunny can connect Saurav to the murder, then we don't ever have to worry about him finding Aarti. This means Aarti and Ayaan will be free. They won't need to hide. But how? How will we get them connected? How will we trace that bastard? How will we ever know who the victim was other than his name?"

Ria, with guilt on her face, said, "Well… this is what I did...the illegal act that I mentioned to you. One of the officers had found a glove. He picked it as evidence but I took it from him saying it's my granny's."

Abeer said, "What's wrong with you Ria? Why did you take the evidence from him? Are you out of your mind?"

Ria sucking a deep breath continued, "It's not something I wanted for myself. It's Bunny's. I needed something of his to trace him. He had worn the pair when he broke the basement door. I don't know how but one of the gloves was on the floor and I thought it's the best way to get back to him." Abeer frowned. She glared at him. He stood up from his chair and walked up to her.

Holding her hands in his, in a commanding voice he said, "Don't even think of it. I will not let you go through it again. Not ever again. I know what it costs you. No. Never ever."

Ria said, "Wow. You think I am acting fussy about the whole thing. It's not a big deal Abeer. It's going to cost Aarti and Ayaan their freedom if I don't trace that guy. They will never be able to go back home. They'll keep hiding forever. Saurav shall find her someday and then what will you do? Do you really think the police can trace him faster than me? Let me do it. Let me do it for myself."

Abeer stared at her blankly. What kind of a woman she was! For her, Aarti and Ayaan were more important than the suffering that she'll go through by holding that evil glove in her hands. And what kind of a man would he be, if he lets her hurt herself just to give freedom to let Aarti and Ayaan live?

Ria spoke, "You don't have a choice, Abeer."

Abeer, angry with himself, "I don't?"

Ria shook her head. Looking straight into his eyes, Ria said, "I will trace him with or without you. But I want you to be with me. I don't want to be alone with him again."

Abeer said, "I'll never let you go close to him. Never ever again in this life."

Ria smiled at him.

Abeer said, "So you won't listen to me? You have made up your mind."

She nodded. Abeer irritated to the core, "Alright then. Promise me you won't come with me. You just tell me his location and I'll handle this without you."

Ria said, "Abeer, you know very well it's not always that easy. Bunny went to so many places with Ayaan. We may find him at one go and we may not. You'll need me to try again on him."

Abeer shook his head, "No. I won't let you come with me..." and then he saw her smile...

His temper blew up. Abeer said, "I can read you like a book Ria. I know you'll follow me if I go alone, right?"

Ria spoke, "Wow. So you think I'll follow you? Why would I do that?"

Abeer said, "I know how your mind works. I may not have your abilities but I surely know what's in that head of yours. You already have everything planned. Don't act stubborn with me." Her expressions changed as she looked at him.

Ria said, "I know I'll be safer with you. What if Bunny comes back here?"

Abeer took a deep breath. He knew she was right. What if he goes looking for him and he changes his plans and comes back to Ria? How will she manage again? We don't get lucky twice. She wasn't safe here. He couldn't leave her alone. He couldn't trust anyone else to take care of her other than himself. He will protect her. He won't fail this time.

Abeer said, "Oh Goddd… How will I manage? How will I concentrate on that ass and you at the same time? You are not safe here. I can't leave you alone Ria."

She nodded her head and said innocently, "Yes Abeer. You are absolutely right." She winked at him. He shook his head in frustration but he knew… he had no choice.

Looking into her eyes, he said, "Fine lady. You win. You are coming along with me. But mind you…you will do as I say and there is no argument in this. Promise me Ria."

Ria giving him the warmest smile ever, "I swear Abeer. Trust me."

****

The cops came. They surveyed the house one last time and left. Ria asked Abeer to get the glove out from the kitchen drawer. She remembered asking the cop to put it in there. Abeer took the glove out and handed it to her. As soon as she took the glove, her hand started trembling. And then… she slipped her hand inside it. He watched her as her expressions changed. She started to get pale. She was shivering. There were droplets of water coming down her face. He watched her helplessly as she used her gift again. He just hoped this time it wouldn't cost her much.

But he was wrong. The physical change she underwent was frightening. Her face was white as snow. Her whole body started to quake. Her eyes were wide open. It seemed as if she was bloodless. He got furious with himself and walked up to her. He held the gloved hand and took out the glove and threw it. She at once started to take deep long breaths. The next moment she rushed into the bathroom and he followed her. He held her as she emptied her stomach due to her body's reaction, which was overtaken by the evil effects of the glove. He slowly got her out of the bathroom and wrapped her with two blankets. She was still shaking. He brought her the relief pills but she refused to gulp them due to the pain in her stomach. But seeing his uncontrollable concern, she took one tablet down her throat.

After many long minutes, she whispered, "He is somewhere nearby. And he is all set to try again." ****
They drove off. Abeer kept looking at Ria every ten seconds. He was worried. She had barely uttered something from her mouth while he kept questioning her. Abeer for the twentieth time, "You sure you fine Ria? You don't look so. I am really worried for you.
You are scaring me to death."

Her temples were paining. Her eyes were heavy. She wanted to speak out and reassure him but had no strength. Her body was too weak with the visions. The reactions were too strong and it hit her badly. She said weakly, "I am fine."

He frowned. He was too concerned about her.

She continued, "We are getting closer. This will affect me more."

Abeer looked at her, "You mean he is here... on this side of the hills?"

Ria nodded and shut her eyes. She started getting cold. With each passing mile, she was shivering even more. Her temples were paining horribly.

She whispered, "Keep driving Abeer. I'll tell you when to take a turn." She kept gesturing with her fingers to the turns.

He was getting restless. He couldn't see her in so much pain. How he craved to take her back to the house and get her some rest! The twisted scene in her vision was making her tremble crazily. She kept directing Abeer with shaky fingers. And then he stopped the car.

Looking at Ria, he gently said, "Open your eyes dear. Is this the place?" She forced her eyelids open and gazed at the bar, right in front of the car.

'The Grapes' Yes, this was the place she had visualized in her last scene. She knew this place but it wasn't the place that met her character. But today she has to go in. Her physical reaction gave her chills as she read the name. With shaky lips, she said, "He is inside."

Abeer went still. He then looked at her and asked, "Bunny D'souza? Here? Now?"

She nodded slowly. He didn't know what to say. He had thought this would take much more time but she had located him. He should be grateful that Ria's suffering will come to an end now but he hadn't expected to find that man so quickly. He had wanted to leave her somewhere safe, somewhere she could rest while he took over Bunny. But now they had no time for this.

And with a stern voice, he said, "Ria. I am going inside and you will not follow me. You stay here and I mean that. Don't forget you had promised me. I am trusting you Ria."

Without another word, he opened his door and slid out. He locked all the four doors of the car.

He then went inside… The Grapes. The interiors were too smoky. It took a few seconds for his eyes to get adjusted to the lights there. He slowly walked to the bar area. The bartender looked at him. He then turned his back to the bar and looked for Bunny. He spotted him drinking alone in the last booth. He went up to the booth and took a place beside him.

Bunny angrily, "What the hell… get out from here…Now."

The man wore a white bandage on his forehead. Abeer was satisfied. Ria had made the bastard suffer with immense pain last night.

Abeer asked softly, "How are you… Bunny D'souza?"

He froze. He then slowly put the glass of beer on the table and stared at Abeer. The man said, "I don't know you man. Who are you? And I think you are mistaken…. I am no Bunny and I don't even know any Bunnys."

Abeer observed, "Oh… amnesia… hmmm… You know it's a funny disease. You never know when the memory is going to come back. Let me help you regain some memories of yours. I am sure I'll be a great help to you. Bunny D'souza, has earlier worked for Saurav of Singapore and is a part of all his crimes. In fact he has also done a kidnapping. Oh… by the way, do you know kidnapping is almost equal to a murder? The charges are gonna be high."

The man eyeing him, "Are you a cop?" He dropped his hands casually under the table.

Abeer advised, "Don't even think of it." He at once took out the gun from his jacket pocket and placed the pointer behind his shoulders. He then asked Bunny to place both his hands on the table and Bunny obeyed him. He stiffened with Abeer's reaction.

Abeer said, "Good. You chose the right thing to do. Now let me answer your question, no, I am not a cop. I am Ayaan's uncle."

Bunny started sweating. He licked his lips nervously.

Abeer clenched his teeth and murmured, "Yes. I am the one man who has all the reasons to see your guts spilling out."

The man got scared as he asked, "But you are not going to kill me, right? Not in front of so many people."

Abeer regretting, "You are right about this Bunny. I really want to kill you. But I won't do that. I know you deserve to die for putting my nephew and my sister through hell. But I didn't come here to shoot you. I have a deal for you. You'll have to go against Saurav and get him behind the bars."

Bunny, with a sarcastic laughter, "You are crazy. I would rather go for a lifetime imprisonment than put the blame on Saurav. At least I'll be alive in prison."

"You have misunderstood your choices", a second voice said. Bunny's eyes became wide, as Ria sat next to him, on the empty side. She didn't even look once at Abeer. She knew he was disgusted seeing her inside the bar. But she couldn't control herself from making the appearance. The reactions that she was having were far stronger than the promise that she had given to him.

Ria said, "Look Bunny. We are not offering you the chance to go to the prison for kidnapping Ayaan." The man was confused. He looked at Ria then at Abeer and then back at Ria. She continued, "The punishment of kidnapping Ayaan would be too little in the prison. Instead we'll just call Saurav and tell him where you are. In fact… we'll also tell him…that you are ready to tell the police that it was him who had ordered you to kill Hasan. You had shot him of course. But will the government leave on such an amazing deal… getting a criminal on their side while they catch the bigger fish who is actually the king of the ocean? Think about it."

Bunny's jaws dropped. He didn't know how to react. He had nowhere to run. Ria continued, "When we describe the murder scene, how you killed him and how Hasan dropped down in the pool of blood, near Saurav's feet, begging for his life, I think Saurav will surely be convinced that it is you who narrated us the murder story. We are sure he would love to see you again…"

Bunny cried. He was shivering with the thought of Saurav. Lowering his voice, he spoke, "I never said a word against him to anyone. I never told my work stories as well."

Abeer said, "You are getting us wrong. It doesn't matter whether you voiced out the secrets. All that matters is that Saurav will believe that you did."

Bunny looked at Abeer and then at Ria. He broke down. Just the thought of facing Saurav gave him jitters. He knew Saurav would kill him. He cried, "My life won't be worth a penny if Saurav gets to know about me."

Ria with a mocking smile, "I wonder what would he do with you if he gets to know you were supposed to deliver a little boy, supposedly his son, the child he never wanted and didn't even know about, to his parents, for a huge sum of money in return."

Bunny was sweating continuously. He was in a state of shock. He couldn't believe how the table turned towards him. She went on, "And then there's always the information we could give him about how and what all you stole from his house. Right Bunny?"

Abeer was also shocked with this information. She had not told him about all this. He was stunned by her perfect declaration. And then he noticed the pale face of hers. She was still shivering, though she tried to keep calm. His gaze dropped to her hand which she held in her lap and he noticed it was covered with a black glove again.

Ria said, "Do you think he'll believe you helped yourself to a few of his assets? I am sure he always thought it was Aarti who fled with all her jewellery and cash. It will be awesome to tell him the truth now. He would love to know that it was you who packed them up after she left. You took them as your payment… for all that you had done for your master. Am I not right Bunny D'souza?"

Bunny pleaded, "Please. Please… do not tell him all this. You can't do that to me. He'll surely kill me. As soon as you call him, he'll sign my death certificate. Please save me from him."

Abeer in a calmed voice, "It's up to you now Bunny. It's your decision. Will you feel safer…if Saurav is in prison or if he is free?

Now…you take the call."

Chapter 12

Abeer asked, "You still look pale, Ria. Are you sure you got enough to eat?"

Ria said, "Hmmm…" She was happily lying down on the couch in his apartment. She added, "I have still not got my appetite back from the plane ride. After landing at Bangalore, I may never eat again."

He grinned, "Well.. I'll need to see that to believe."

He surveyed her. She seemed to be perfectly fine. Just a little tired. The past week had been terrible for her. They had convinced Bunny to spill out everything about his former boss to the CBI. Of course, the best way to stay alive was to go against Saurav. And he did that. He was granted immunity from the prosecution for his own involvement. The CBI agents were delighted to get their hands on Saurav. They arrested him with the charges of murder and dishonest crimes. Aarti also helped the cops in locating a few pieces of evidence at her former house. Both Abeer and Ria were sure that Saurav won't be spared this time.

He had enough evidence against him.

Ria quietly, "Will Aarti be called to court?"

Abeer said, "I hope not. Bunny is enough to get Saurav behind the bars. He'll be there for a good number of years."

Ria said, "Thank God his bail has been denied. Aarti doesn't have to worry about him anymore."

Abeer, with a satisfying tone, "As soon as he is behind the bars for good, we can start the divorce proceedings. It won't be difficult to get him to sign the papers."

He took a deep breath and continued, "At last, Aarti will be free to live. She would finally get rid of her fears. She and Ayaan would be free to live in peace."

Ria asked, "And what about Ramya and Bunny?"

Abeer said, "Bunny will face charges for kidnapping. Ramya has signed against him, so he'll too need to be punished though not as much as Saurav. And Ramya… she'll get a shorter imprisonment as she was just a helper for Ayaan. But I am grateful, now the three of them shall not dare return to our lives."

He gazed at her. He was delighted to have her in his apartment. He smiled to himself as he saw her getting comfortable on the couch. It was just perfect for her. Her soft shiny long hair was all over the couch. He possessed them. He had always listened to his instincts. They never failed him. He never questioned his instinct to bring her with him or the one urging him to keep her here, with him. He had lived all his life following that instinct. And he knew, it will not fail him now as well. Ria looked at his apartment. The space was huge. It was well maintained with perfect décor. It was designed with chic comfort in mind and she was sure Abeer had done the interiors himself. It was just like him. Too perfect. There was no reason for her to accompany him to Bangalore. But he got her with him. She didn't argue or question him. Everything was taken care of. Yes, she wanted to spend as much time as she could with him. But now everything is over. And now she needed the answer, "Why am I here Abeer?"

As soon as she questioned him, his face lost all the colours. He was expressionless. He knew she read him well. But now he was all blank. Abeer said, "You need good rest Ria. And I can't take a chance. I can't trust you to take care of yourself. So don't you argue with me. I have watched how the visions react to you physically and in the past few weeks you have repeatedly gone through it. You have never been so stressed. You need to fully recover."

Ria said, "So that means once I have fully recovered, I can go back home?"

He frowned. His temper rose up. How could she do it again? How could she make plans to leave him again? Earlier too she didn't give him a chance to explain what he wanted and now again she is doing the same. Very coolly she had announced her plans and left him. Today she is again in a cool mind and repeating the same. She really had the guts to leave him again but no... he won't let this happen to him. Not again. Never ever again. He stood up from his chair and went up to the couch where she laid. Seeing him coming towards her, she sat down. He took a place close to her, very close to her.

He fingered her jaw and then felt the pulse hammering. He smiled. Looking into her eyes, Abeer said, "You can try to pretend Ria but you can't hide the reactions when I touch you."

The sparks of electricity beneath his fingers warmed her. He covered her lips with his, forcing even a greater reaction. Her response was immediate. She helplessly kissed him. He pushed her top up and covered his palms with the lacy breasts. Their mouths twisted together. Their breathing grew. After a few long minutes, he parted with her lips and looked at her. Her lips were swollen and her eyes were shut. Her nipples wanted to tear off the laces around them.

Kissing her breasts, he said, "I am sure you won't like to go back to the hills, to your house Ria. I know you don't want to leave me. I too want you to stay. I know you love me. A woman like you will never make love to a man otherwise. You won't."

His mouth was on her neck now. He tongued it and she shivered. He demanded, "Tell me. Tell me, you love me."

Ria, relishing the chance to be free with her words, whispered, "I do. I love you Abeer." The words had barely escaped her before his mouth covered hers, thirstily drinking the words from her lips.

Abeer said, "Stay with me Ria. Forever. Marry me. Please." She opened her eyes and looked at him. Ria asked, "Marriage? You don't want to marry me Abeer."

Abeer said, "Sweetheart. You are supposed to be a physic. By now you should have known what I want."

Her throat ached. With emotions she spoke, "I knew how you felt the moment you took me in your arms when you came to look for me at my house, the night Bunny broke in. And I also know what you feel about…my gift. You have spent your life, shielding your thoughts and feelings from the whole world. And I know, you hate it when I read them, by just touching you."

He bluntly said, "I don't like it. I agree. It will take some time for me to adjust to it. But I know one thing, that your ability works differently with me but not with the others. You respond everytime I touch you. Your emotions are more powerful than your abilities Ria. The closer we get, it becomes more difficult for you to concentrate on anything else other than what I make you feel."

He slowly moved his hands behind her back and touched her nape. Shivers ran down her spine and she hugged him tightly. He whispered, "I may not always like the power of your gift but I love the effect my touch has on you. We both have the same effect when we touch each other."

She moved back and said, "I am not normal Abeer. I know this. I have accepted it long back. I can't even live in a city. I am scared to be in a crowd. The thought of being among a small crowd makes me feel sick. I can't even walk on the streets. I can't even shield myself. It's not possible. Let me go."

He listened to every word of hers. He held her hands and softly spoke, "We can live anywhere you feel comfortable. Shimla is not the only place. There are many other mountains in the country. There are beaches. You name it and we'll live there. I promise. I want to live with you."

He bit her earlobe and she moaned. He then smoothened it with the tip of his tongue. Abeer said, "Just say you want to stay back. Please say you want to marry me. I'll do anything for you."

She had made peace with her abilities. She knew she had to give away the intimacy and love in her life. But to be offered it now, from the man she loved, was the most precious gift she could have ever received. "Yes", she said calmly.

Her throat was too full. The one word made his eyes fill up with emotions he never knew existed. He sat up and scooped her into his arms. He carried her to his bedroom and swiftly made her lie on the bed. He lay beside her and looked at her. The sensuality of having her in his bedroom made him shiver. He hurriedly took off all her clothes and threw them unattended. She, with battling fingers, opened his buttons and zipped down his pants. He removed them with one go. He slowly followed her down. With one forefinger he traced her lips and her delicate jaw. In a husky voice, Abeer said, "I love you Ria Mehta".

She smiled her secret smile and whispered, "I know."

He suddenly laughed and surprised her by saying, "You think you know everything, right? But that's not correct. Let me tell you lady, you are not the only one to get the visions. I have had one myself. Over and over... of you and me... on this bed. Just like this."

Her eyes widened in surprise and she gave her best smile to him. He watched her with his half opened eyes. He had the most beautiful girl in his arms and they shall never part.

Her soft long silky hair spilled across the sheets. Her skin was shining like diamonds. The black sheets were perfect for her divine body. He lowered his head to kiss her. They both knew… this was one vision that would last forever… and ever.

The End

About the Author

Aditi Agarwal Poddar, who writes under the pseudonym of Pakhi, is an entrepreneur by profession and a writer by choice. She has her own Events Company and also a manufacturing unit of wooden artifacts. Her first book, **Love Me Again**, has given her the privilege of winning four prestigious award to her kitty. Kolmo most Creative, Kolmo Rising Star, Literoma Best Debut Author of 2019 and Literoma Nari Samman 2020, making her readers really proud of her.

Her second title, **Strings of Love** published in the year 2020, and her third title, **Invincible Love** published in the year 2022 also received much accolade.

She is a social butterfly and a tale teller who has touched the hearts of hundreds of readers on the social media. She is a believer of love more than destiny. High optimism and spirituality is what keeps her going. She believes 'Rising in love' is far more important than 'Falling in love'. For her, self love is greater than the love that exists for another.

Erotica writer as the readers have named her, she is loved especially for the soaring temperatures with her vivid descriptions. She is also described as a holder of Ph. D in Romance by her readers.

Other Titles by the Author are:

LOVE ME AGAIN
https://www.amazon.in/Again
AditiAgarwaPoddar
Pakhi/dp/1647832330/

STRINGS OF LOVE
https://www.amazon.in/Strings
PakhiAditiAgarwal
Poddar/dp/1648928838/

INVINCIBLE LOVE
https://amzn.eu/d/dHWn6KK

www.ingramcontent.com/pod-product-compliance
Lightning Source LLC
Chambersburg PA
CBHW020550160726
47991CB00002B/674